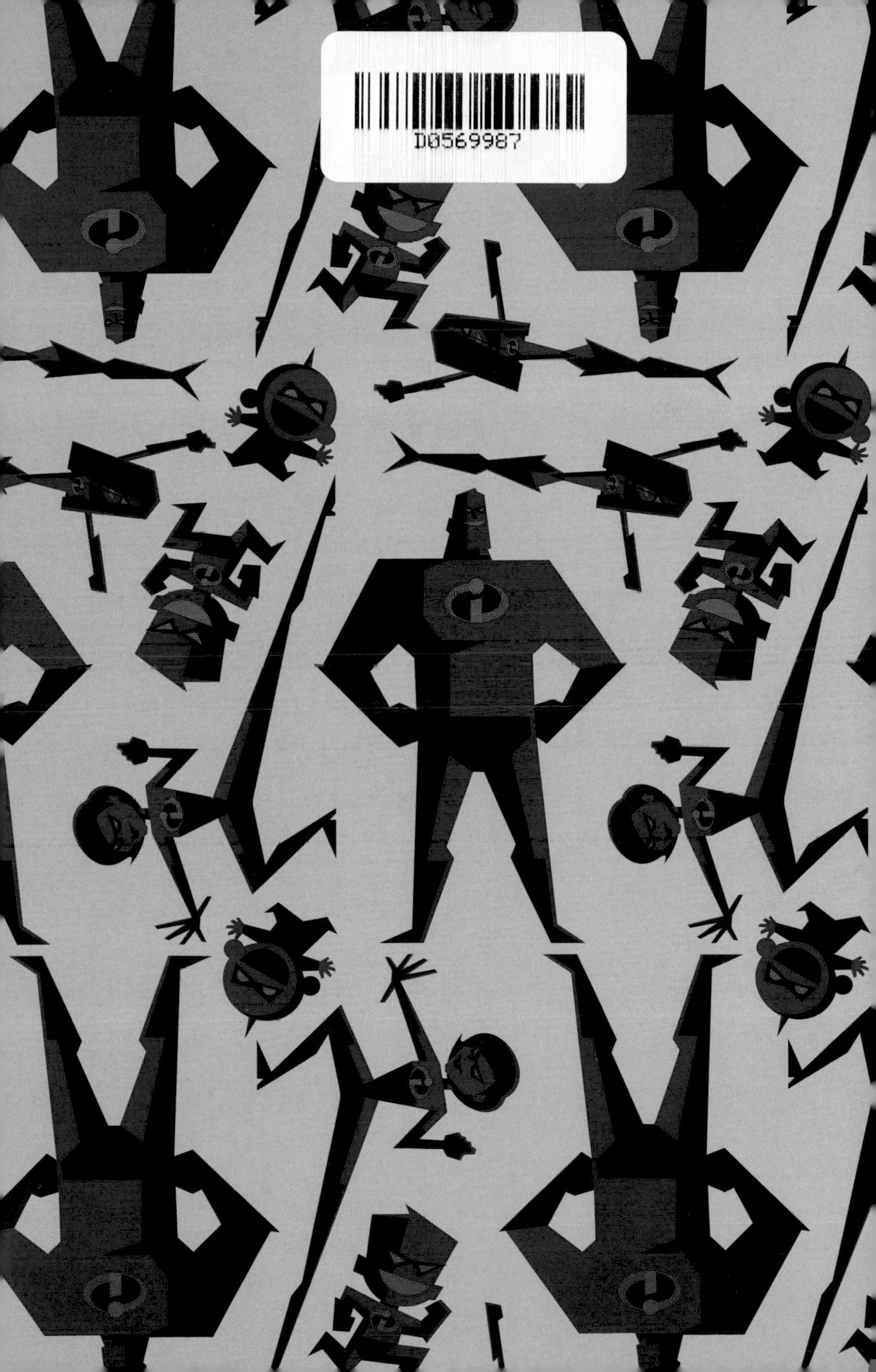

ALSO FROM JOE BOOKS

Disney•Pixar Inside Out Cinestory Comic
Disney Big Hero 6 Cinestory Comic
Disney Zootopia Cinestory Comic
Disney•Pixar Finding Nemo Cinestory Comic
Disney•Pixar Finding Dory Cinestory Comic
Disney•Pixar Cars Cinestory Comic
Disney•Pixar Cars 3 Cinestory Comic
Disney•Pixar Coco Cinestory Comic
Disney Big Hero 6: The Series Cinestory Comic
Disney DuckTales Cinestory Comic
Disney•Pixar The Incredibles Cinestory Comic

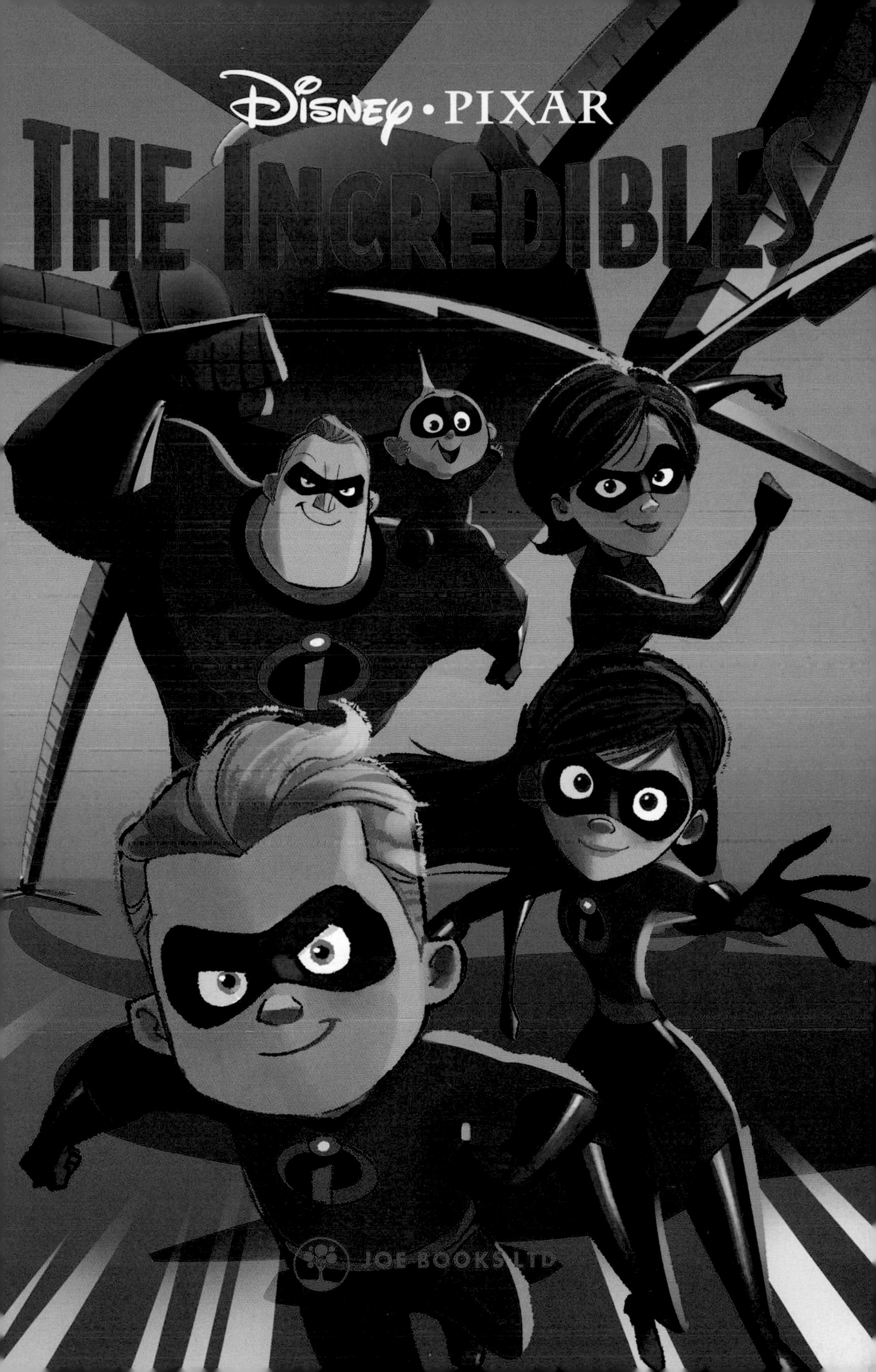
Disney • PIXAR
THE INCREDIBLES
JOE BOOKS LTD

Published in the United States and Canada by Joe Books Ltd.
Copyright © Disney. All rights reserved.

No part of this publication may be reproduced, stored in a
retrieval system, or transmitted in any form or by any means without the express written
permission of the copyright holder.

First Joe Books edition: May 2018

Print ISBN: 978-1-77275-549-7

Names, characters, places, and incidents featured in this publication are
either the product of the author's imagination or are used fictitiously.
Any resemblance to actual persons (living or dead), events, institutions,
or locales, without satiric intent, is coincidental.

Joe Books™ is a trademark of Joe Books Ltd. Joe Books® and the
Joe Books logo are trademarks of Joe Books Ltd, registered in
various categories and countries. All rights reserved.

Library and Archives Canada Cataloguing in Publication
information is available upon request.

Printed and bound in Canada
1 3 5 7 9 10 8 6 4 2

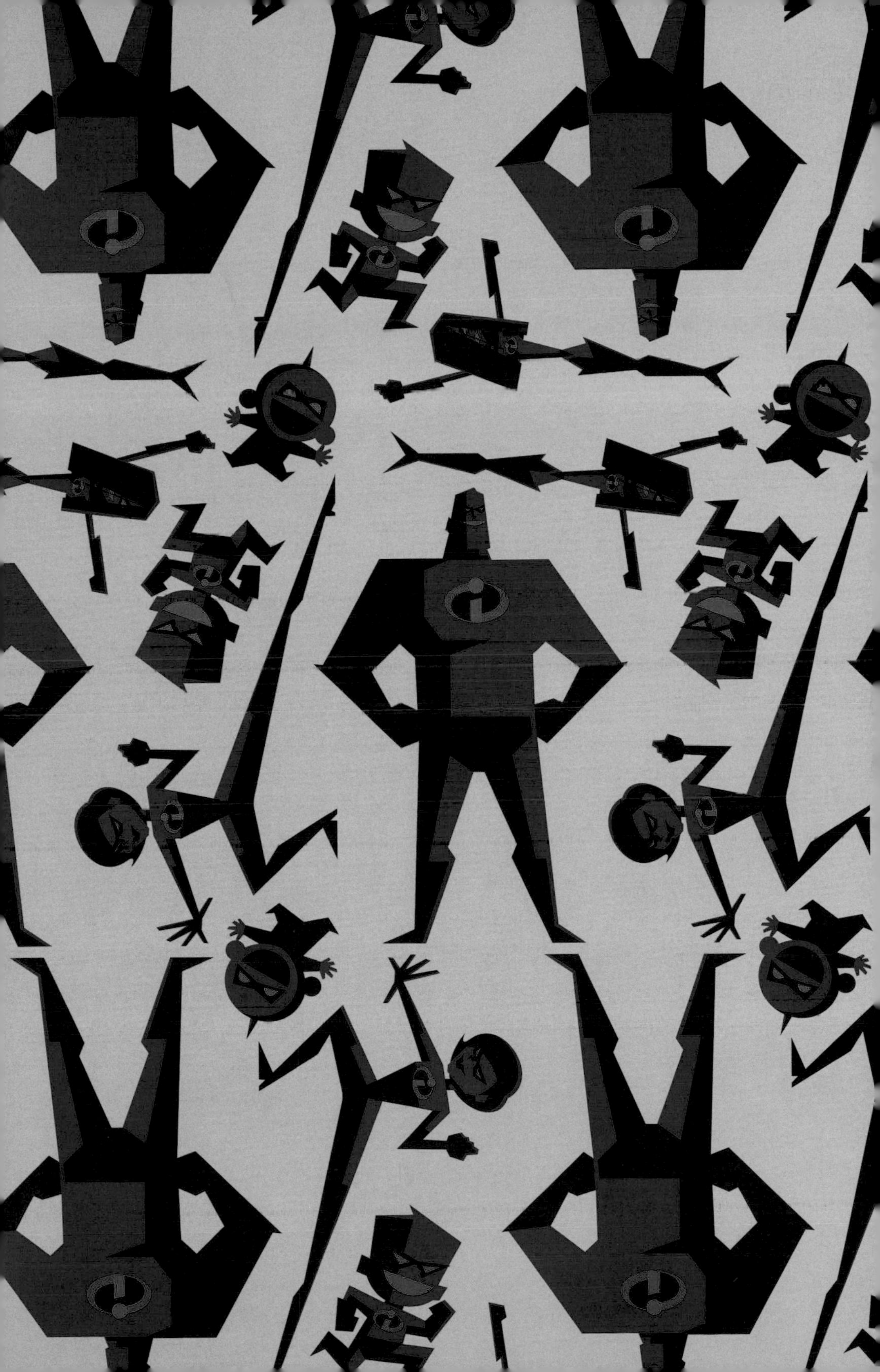

MEET THE INCREDIBLES

A truly super family, the Incredibles might lead normal lives, but they actually possess exceptional powers. How long will the peace and quiet last? Until it's time to save the world and be the heroes they are!

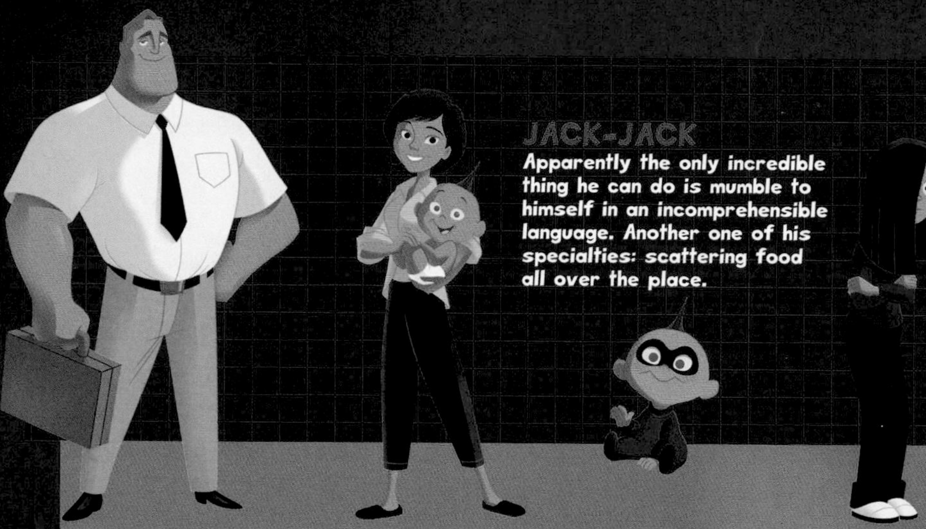

JACK-JACK

Apparently the only incredible thing he can do is mumble to himself in an incomprehensible language. Another one of his specialties: scattering food all over the place.

BOB PARR
(MR. INCREDIBLE)

He works for an insurance company. His previous job: famous Superhero. Now he is a tad overweight and a bit nostalgic.

HELEN PARR
(ELASTIGIRL)

Elastigirl or mom? She's actually both. In any case, taking care of her children is a (very hard) job, and her flexibility makes her great at it.

VIOLET

Like most teenagers, Violet is shy, but unlike typical teens, she can become invisible and create protective force fields around her.

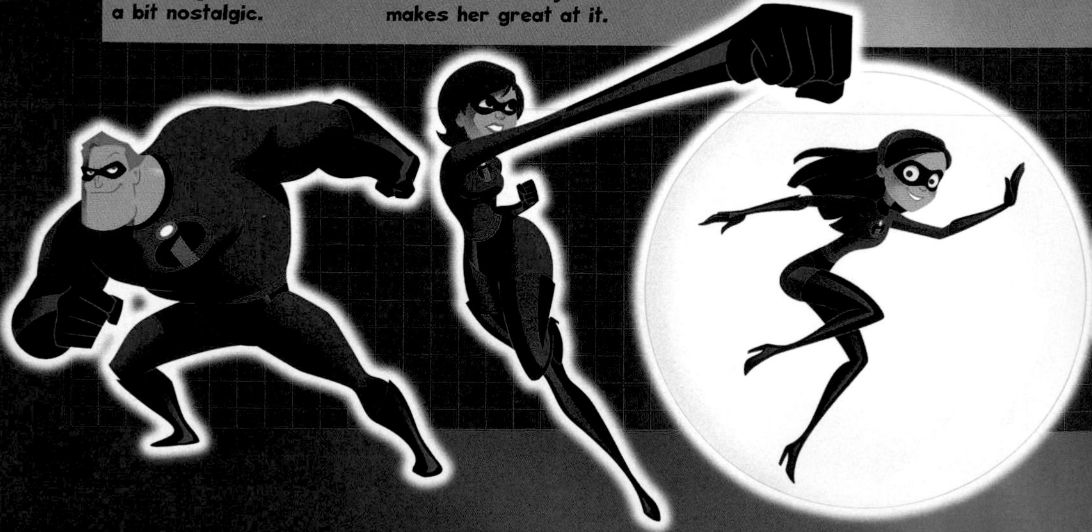

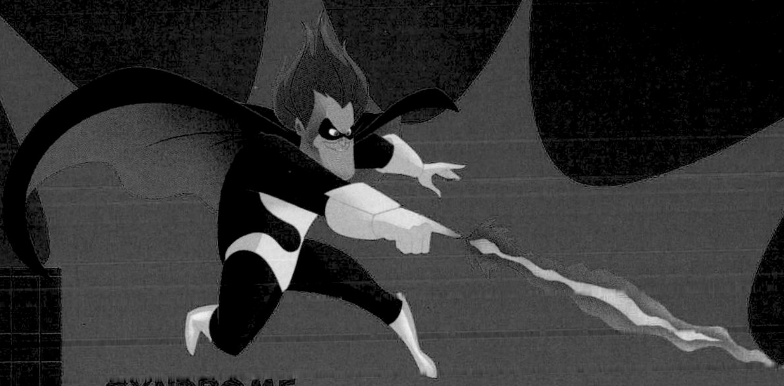

SYNDROME
(BUDDY)
He went from being Mr. Incredible's biggest young fan to his enemy when Mr. Incredible wouldn't join up with him to fight crime. Syndrome became a villain, and his newest project involves an intelligent robotic weapon that can destroy the world.

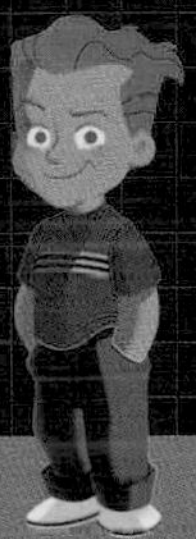

DASH
As an active boy, he's always on the move. Dash's Super power is super speed, and it's impossible to catch up to him.

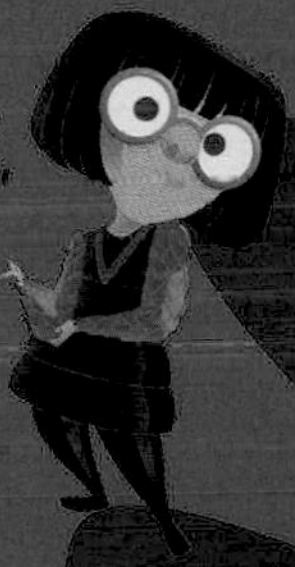

E
(EDNA MODE)
A trend-setting fashion designer and style guru, Edna designs the very stylish Supersuits for the Incredibles. She's very wise, with lots of advice, such as: no capes! The best pro in the business. That's why she's sought out by those who want Super clothes...

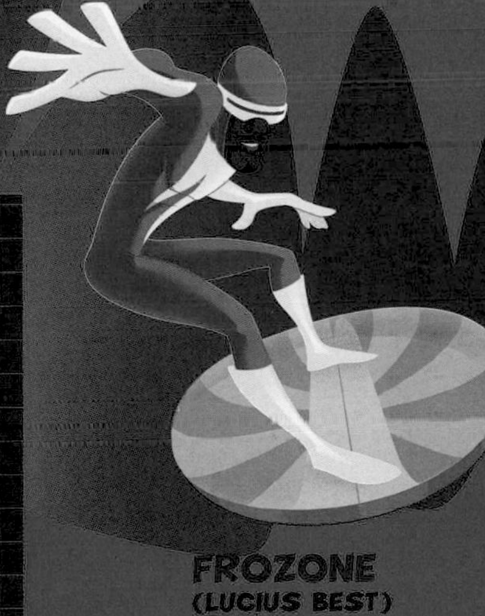

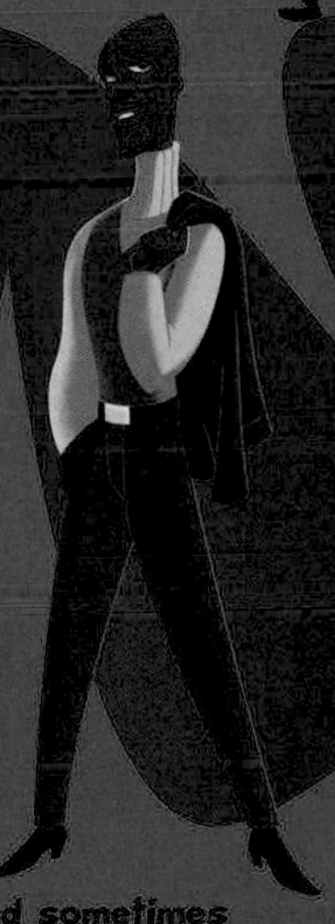

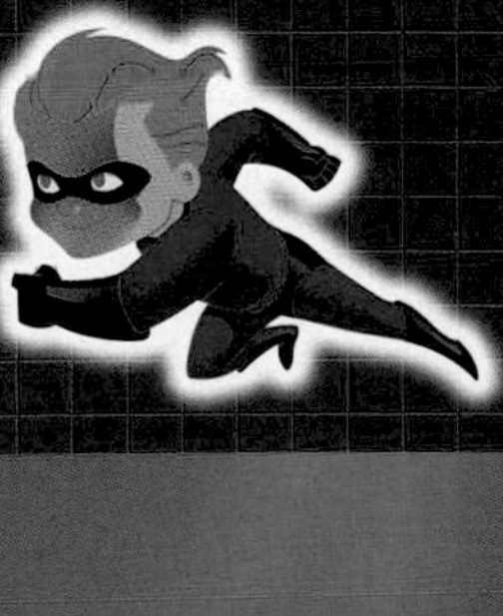

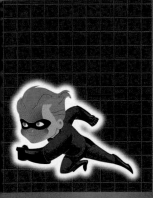

FROZONE
(LUCIUS BEST)
Bob's best friend is witty, and sometimes has an icy sense of humor...literally. In fact, he conceals a power that seems made for him: he can create ice simply by drawing humidity from the air.

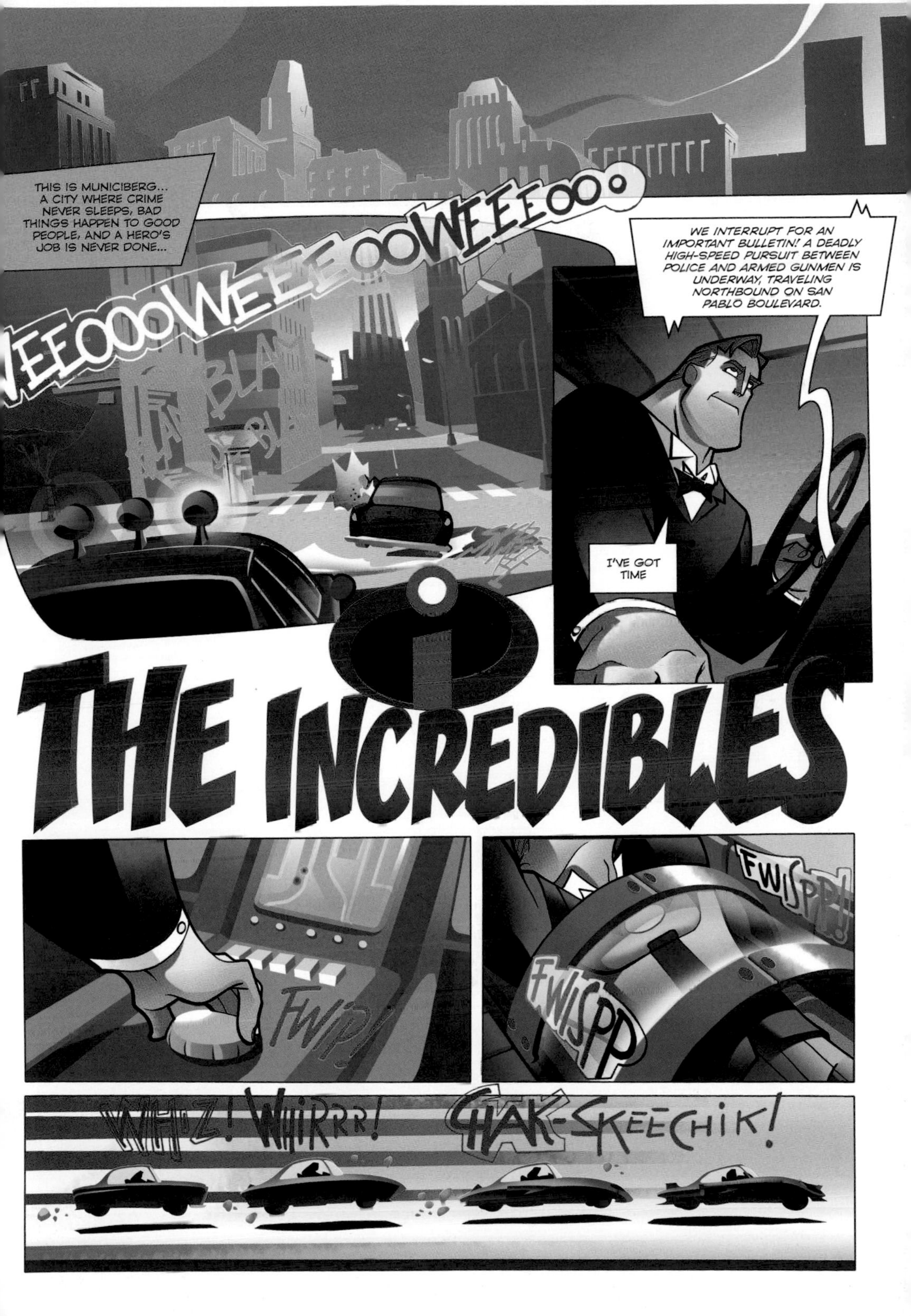
THIS IS MUNICIBERG... A CITY WHERE CRIME NEVER SLEEPS, BAD THINGS HAPPEN TO GOOD PEOPLE, AND A HERO'S JOB IS NEVER DONE...
WEEOOOWEEEOOWEEEOOO
WE INTERRUPT FOR AN IMPORTANT BULLETIN! A DEADLY HIGH-SPEED PURSUIT BETWEEN POLICE AND ARMED GUNMEN IS UNDERWAY, TRAVELING NORTHBOUND ON SAN PABLO BOULEVARD.
I'VE GOT TIME
THE INCREDIBLES
FWIP!
FWISPP!
FWISPP
WHIZ! WHIRRR! CHAK-SKEECHIK!

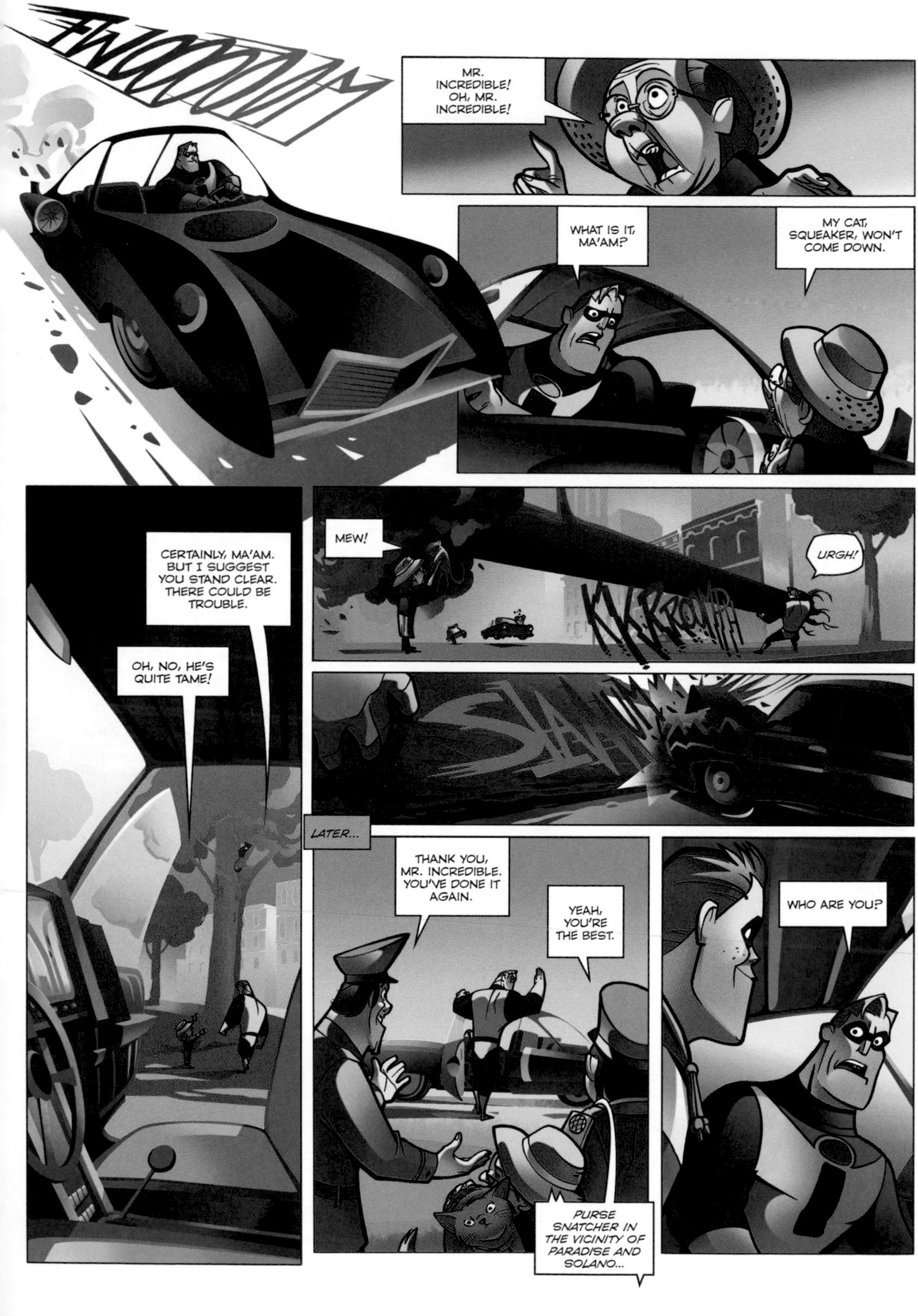
FWOOOOOM
MR. INCREDIBLE! OH, MR. INCREDIBLE!
WHAT IS IT, MA'AM?
MY CAT, SQUEAKER, WON'T COME DOWN.
CERTAINLY, MA'AM. BUT I SUGGEST YOU STAND CLEAR. THERE COULD BE TROUBLE.
OH, NO, HE'S QUITE TAME!
MEW!
URGH!
KKKROUNCH
SLAM
LATER...
THANK YOU, MR. INCREDIBLE. YOU'VE DONE IT AGAIN.
YEAH, YOU'RE THE BEST.
PURSE SNATCHER IN THE VICINITY OF PARADISE AND SOLANO...
WHO ARE YOU?

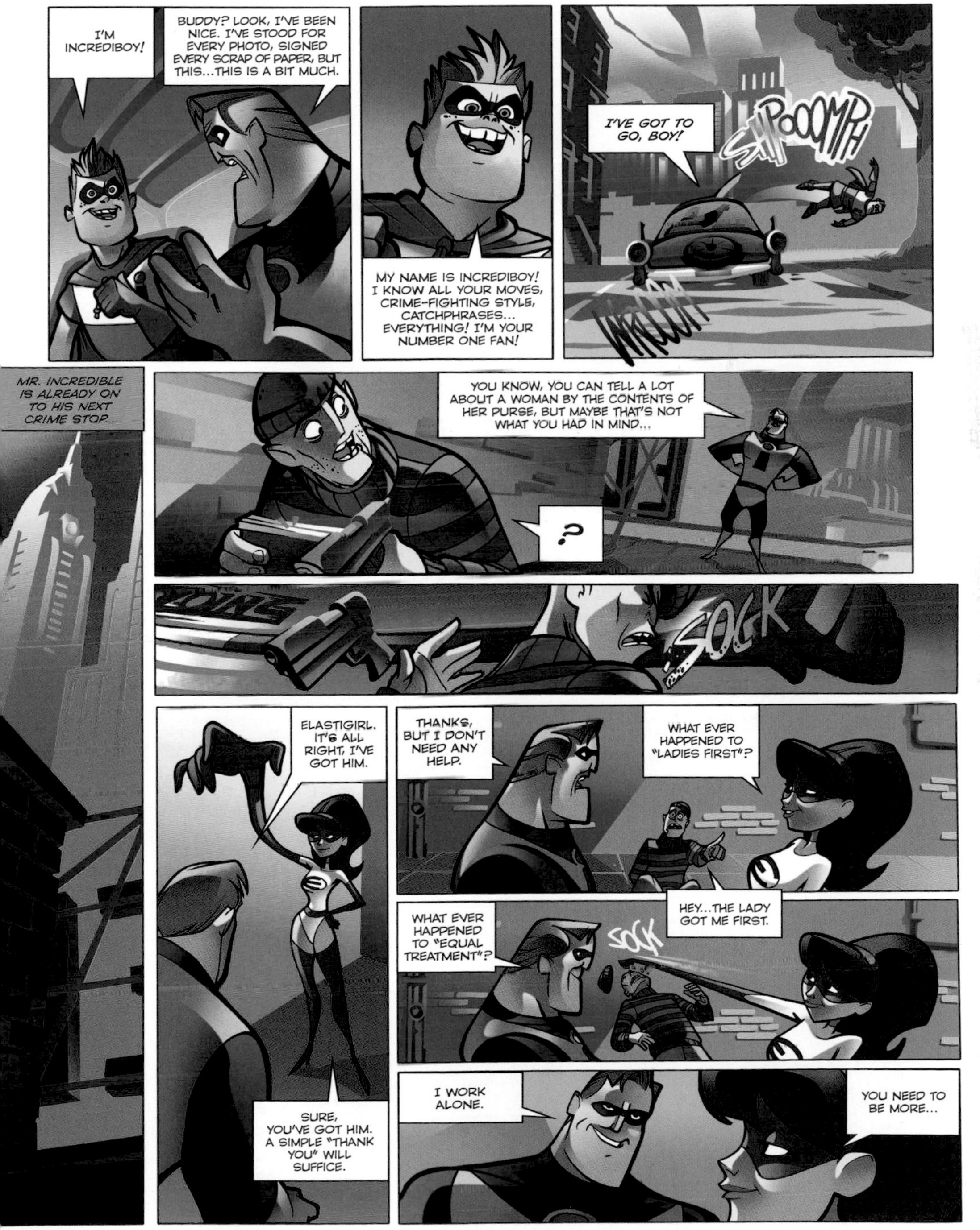
I'M INCREDIBOY!
BUDDY? LOOK, I'VE BEEN NICE. I'VE STOOD FOR EVERY PHOTO, SIGNED EVERY SCRAP OF PAPER, BUT THIS...THIS IS A BIT MUCH.
MY NAME IS INCREDIBOY! I KNOW ALL YOUR MOVES, CRIME-FIGHTING STYLE, CATCHPHRASES... EVERYTHING! I'M YOUR NUMBER ONE FAN!
I'VE GOT TO GO, BOY!
SHPOOOMPH
MR. INCREDIBLE IS ALREADY ON TO HIS NEXT CRIME STOP...
YOU KNOW, YOU CAN TELL A LOT ABOUT A WOMAN BY THE CONTENTS OF HER PURSE, BUT MAYBE THAT'S NOT WHAT YOU HAD IN MIND...
?
SOCK
ELASTIGIRL, IT'S ALL RIGHT, I'VE GOT HIM.
SURE, YOU'VE GOT HIM. A SIMPLE "THANK YOU" WILL SUFFICE.
THANKS, BUT I DON'T NEED ANY HELP.
WHAT EVER HAPPENED TO "LADIES FIRST"?
WHAT EVER HAPPENED TO "EQUAL TREATMENT"?
HEY...THE LADY GOT ME FIRST.
SOCK
I WORK ALONE.
YOU NEED TO BE MORE...

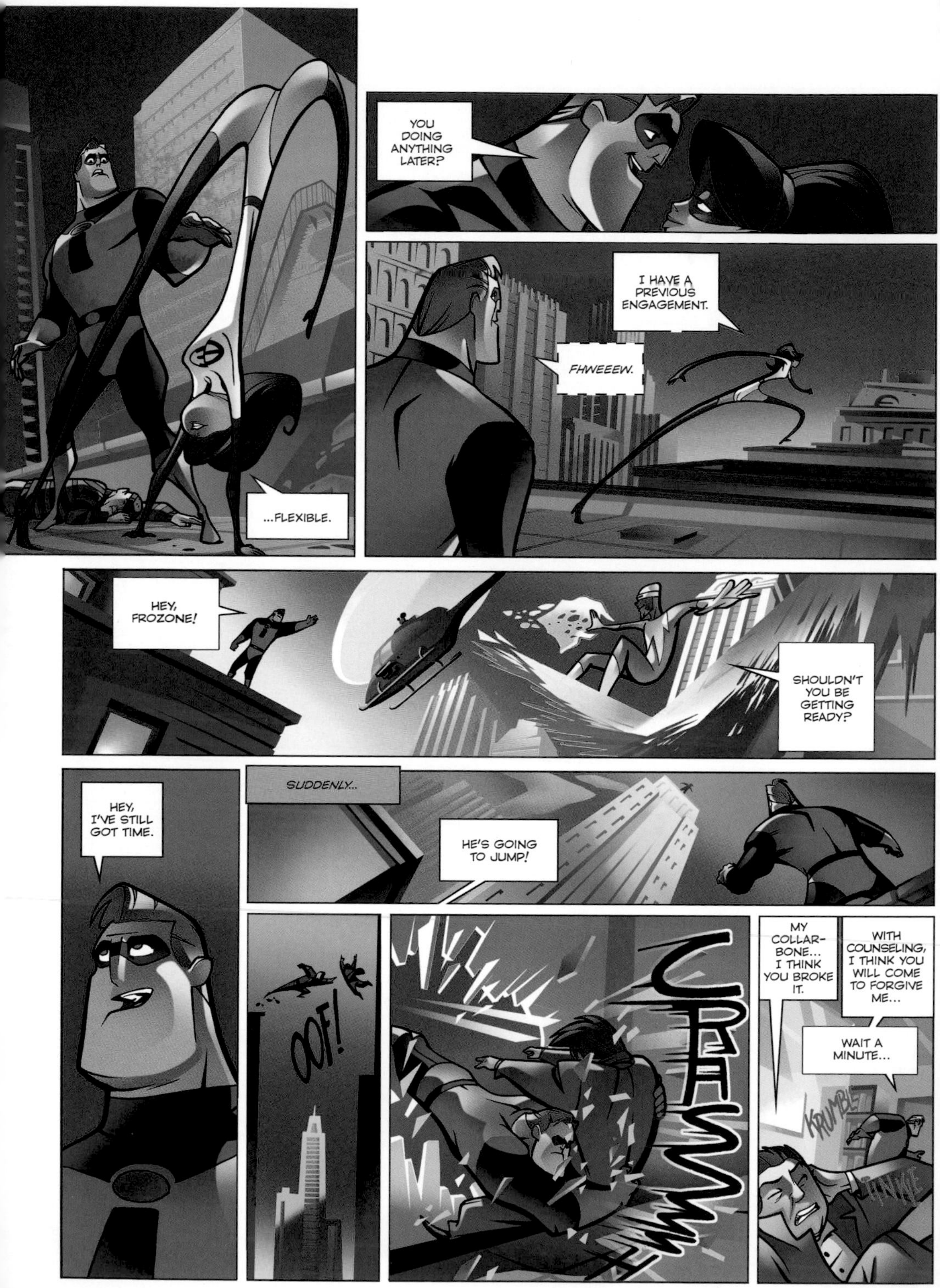
...FLEXIBLE.
YOU DOING ANYTHING LATER?
I HAVE A PREVIOUS ENGAGEMENT.
FHWEEEW.
HEY, FROZONE!
SHOULDN'T YOU BE GETTING READY?
HEY, I'VE STILL GOT TIME.
SUDDENLY...
HE'S GOING TO JUMP!
OOF!
CRASH
MY COLLAR-BONE... I THINK YOU BROKE IT.
WITH COUNSELING, I THINK YOU WILL COME TO FORGIVE ME...
WAIT A MINUTE...
KRUMBLE

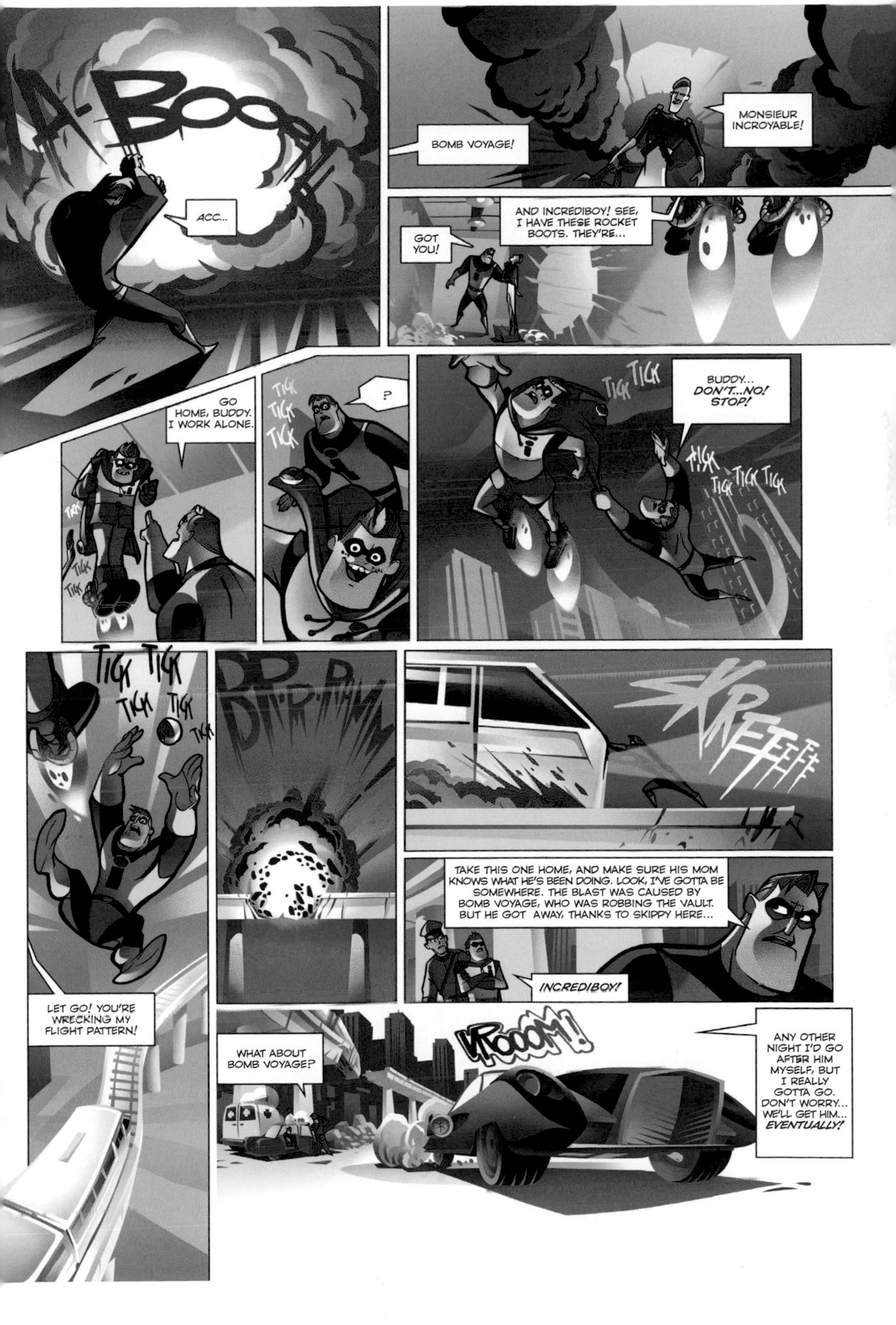
KA-BOOM
ACC...
BOMB VOYAGE!
MONSIEUR INCROYABLE!
GOT YOU!
AND INCREDIBOY! SEE, I HAVE THESE ROCKET BOOTS. THEY'RE...
GO HOME, BUDDY. I WORK ALONE.
TICK TICK TICK
TICK TICK TICK
?
TICK TICK
BUDDY... DON'T...NO! STOP!
TICK TICK TICK TICK
TICK TICK TICK TICK TICK
LET GO! YOU'RE WRECKING MY FLIGHT PATTERN!
SKREEEE
TAKE THIS ONE HOME, AND MAKE SURE HIS MOM KNOWS WHAT HE'S BEEN DOING. LOOK, I'VE GOTTA BE SOMEWHERE. THE BLAST WAS CAUSED BY BOMB VOYAGE, WHO WAS ROBBING THE VAULT. BUT HE GOT AWAY, THANKS TO SKIPPY HERE...
INCREDIBOY!
WHAT ABOUT BOMB VOYAGE?
VROOOM!
ANY OTHER NIGHT I'D GO AFTER HIM MYSELF, BUT I REALLY GOTTA GO. DON'T WORRY... WE'LL GET HIM... EVENTUALLY!

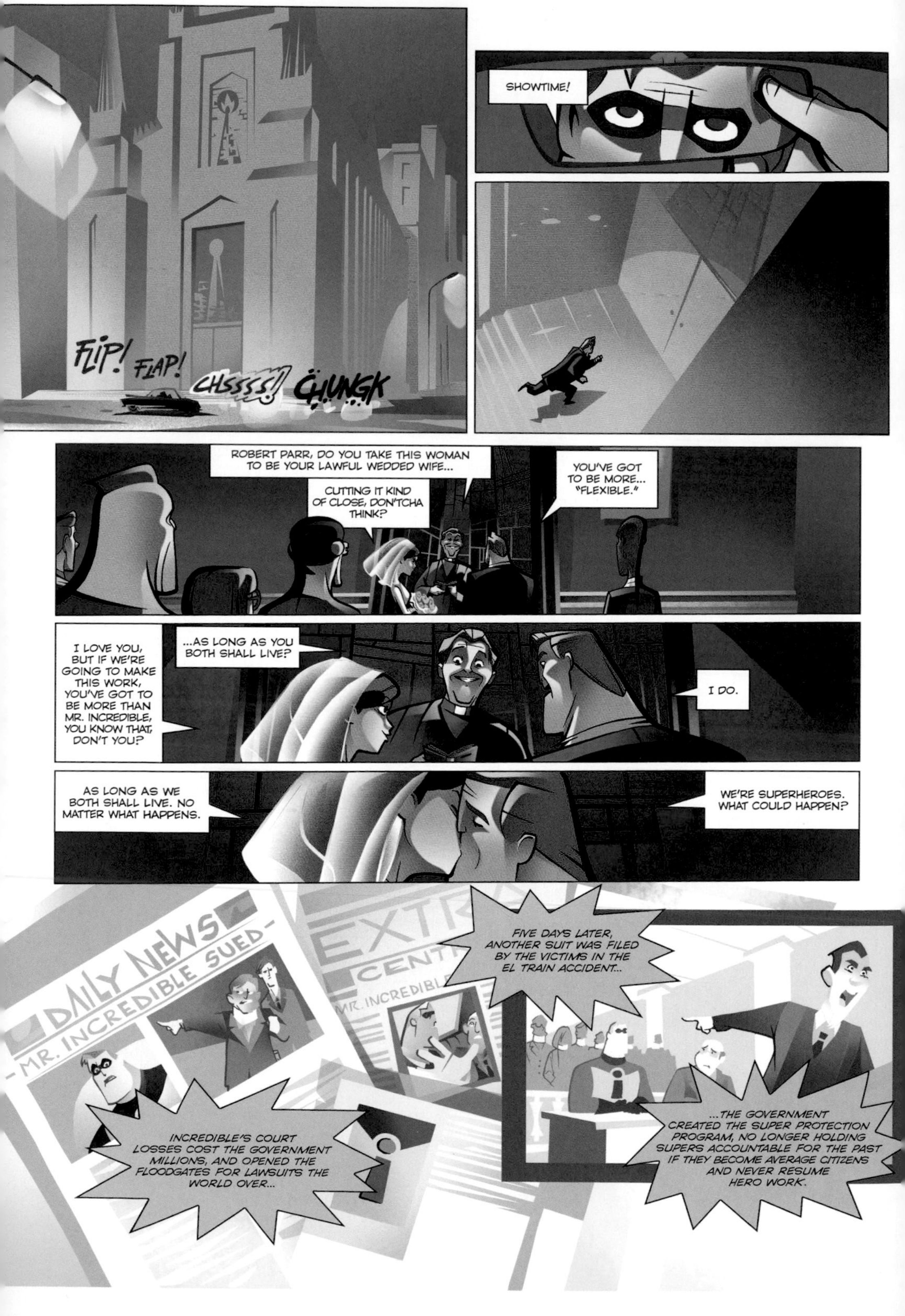

FLIP!
FLAP!
CHSSSS!
CHUNGK
SHOWTIME!
ROBERT PARR, DO YOU TAKE THIS WOMAN TO BE YOUR LAWFUL WEDDED WIFE...
CUTTING IT KIND OF CLOSE, DON'TCHA THINK?
YOU'VE GOT TO BE MORE... "FLEXIBLE."
I LOVE YOU, BUT IF WE'RE GOING TO MAKE THIS WORK, YOU'VE GOT TO BE MORE THAN MR. INCREDIBLE, YOU KNOW THAT, DON'T YOU?
...AS LONG AS YOU BOTH SHALL LIVE?
I DO.
AS LONG AS WE BOTH SHALL LIVE. NO MATTER WHAT HAPPENS.
WE'RE SUPERHEROES. WHAT COULD HAPPEN?
DAILY NEWS
MR. INCREDIBLE SUED
EXTR
CENT
MR. INCREDIBL
FIVE DAYS LATER, ANOTHER SUIT WAS FILED BY THE VICTIMS IN THE EL TRAIN ACCIDENT...
INCREDIBLE'S COURT LOSSES COST THE GOVERNMENT MILLIONS, AND OPENED THE FLOODGATES FOR LAWSUITS THE WORLD OVER...
...THE GOVERNMENT CREATED THE SUPER PROTECTION PROGRAM, NO LONGER HOLDING SUPERS ACCOUNTABLE FOR THE PAST IF THEY BECOME AVERAGE CITIZENS AND NEVER RESUME HERO WORK.

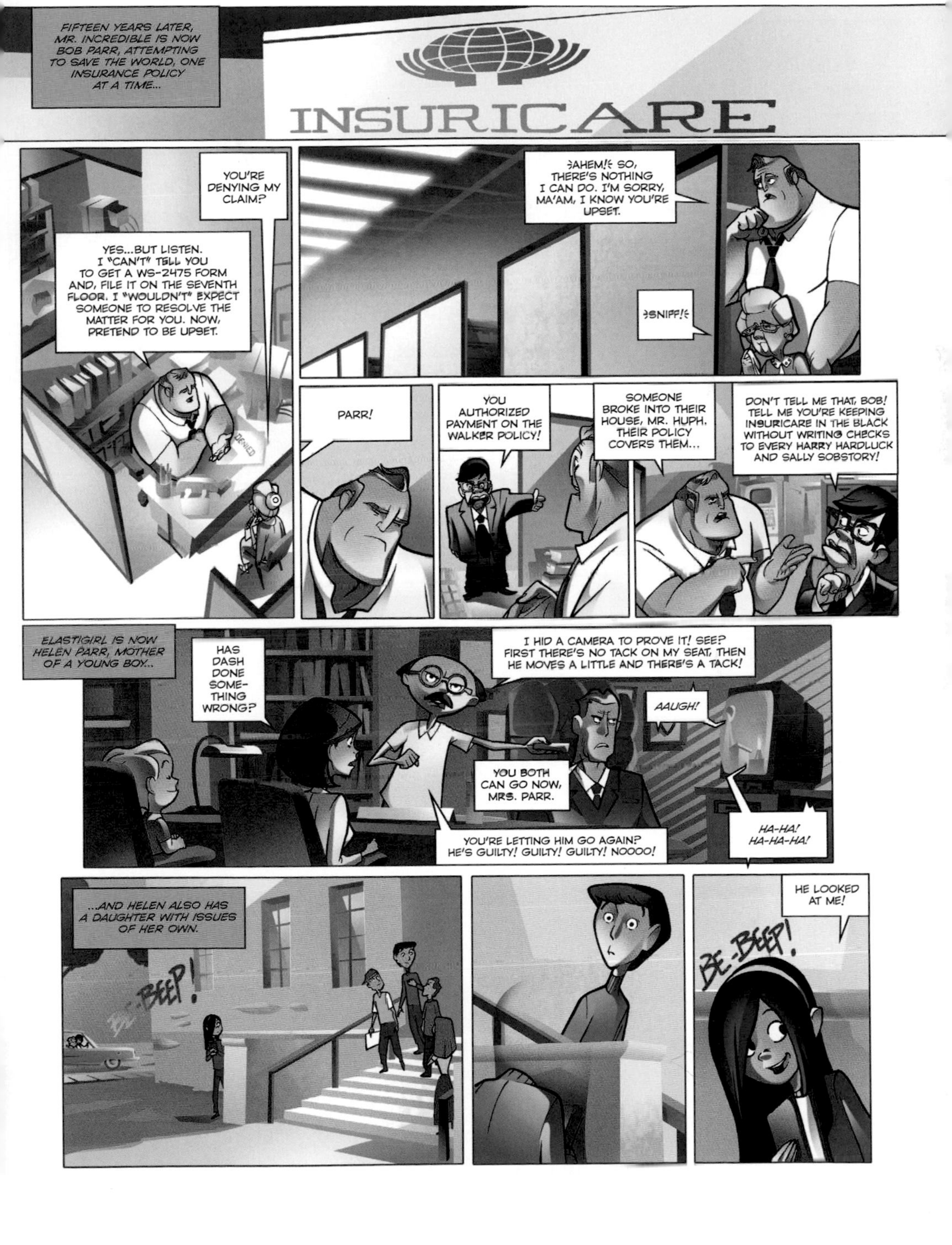
FIFTEEN YEARS LATER, MR. INCREDIBLE IS NOW BOB PARR, ATTEMPTING TO SAVE THE WORLD, ONE INSURANCE POLICY AT A TIME...
INSURICARE
YOU'RE DENYING MY CLAIM?
YES...BUT LISTEN. I "CAN'T" TELL YOU TO GET A WS-2475 FORM AND, FILE IT ON THE SEVENTH FLOOR. I "WOULDN'T" EXPECT SOMEONE TO RESOLVE THE MATTER FOR YOU. NOW, PRETEND TO BE UPSET.
DENIED
AHEM! SO, THERE'S NOTHING I CAN DO. I'M SORRY, MA'AM, I KNOW YOU'RE UPSET.
SNIFF!
PARR!
YOU AUTHORIZED PAYMENT ON THE WALKER POLICY!
SOMEONE BROKE INTO THEIR HOUSE, MR. HUPH. THEIR POLICY COVERS THEM...
DON'T TELL ME THAT, BOB! TELL ME YOU'RE KEEPING INSURICARE IN THE BLACK WITHOUT WRITING CHECKS TO EVERY HARRY HARDLUCK AND SALLY SOBSTORY!
ELASTIGIRL IS NOW HELEN PARR, MOTHER OF A YOUNG BOY...
HAS DASH DONE SOME-THING WRONG?
I HID A CAMERA TO PROVE IT! SEE? FIRST THERE'S NO TACK ON MY SEAT, THEN HE MOVES A LITTLE AND THERE'S A TACK!
AAUGH!
YOU BOTH CAN GO NOW, MRS. PARR.
YOU'RE LETTING HIM GO AGAIN? HE'S GUILTY! GUILTY! GUILTY! NOOOO!
HA-HA! HA-HA-HA!
...AND HELEN ALSO HAS A DAUGHTER WITH ISSUES OF HER OWN.
BE-BEEP!
BE-BEEP!
HE LOOKED AT ME!

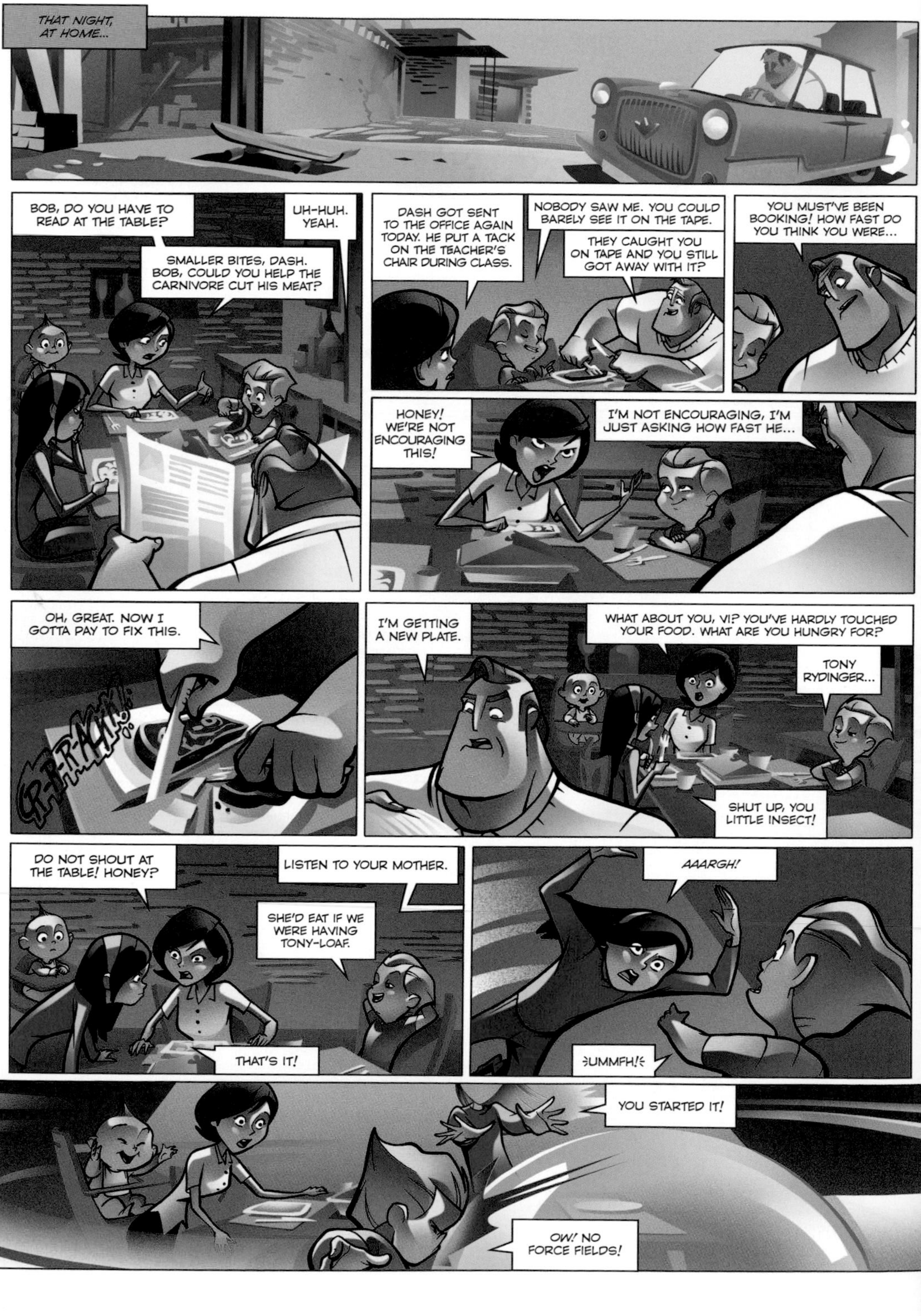
THAT NIGHT, AT HOME...
BOB, DO YOU HAVE TO READ AT THE TABLE?
UH-HUH. YEAH.
SMALLER BITES, DASH. BOB, COULD YOU HELP THE CARNIVORE CUT HIS MEAT?
DASH GOT SENT TO THE OFFICE AGAIN TODAY. HE PUT A TACK ON THE TEACHER'S CHAIR DURING CLASS.
NOBODY SAW ME. YOU COULD BARELY SEE IT ON THE TAPE.
THEY CAUGHT YOU ON TAPE AND YOU STILL GOT AWAY WITH IT?
YOU MUST'VE BEEN BOOKING! HOW FAST DO YOU THINK YOU WERE...
HONEY! WE'RE NOT ENCOURAGING THIS!
I'M NOT ENCOURAGING, I'M JUST ASKING HOW FAST HE...
OH, GREAT. NOW I GOTTA PAY TO FIX THIS.
GR-R-R-AKK!
I'M GETTING A NEW PLATE.
WHAT ABOUT YOU, VI? YOU'VE HARDLY TOUCHED YOUR FOOD. WHAT ARE YOU HUNGRY FOR?
TONY RYDINGER...
SHUT UP, YOU LITTLE INSECT!
DO NOT SHOUT AT THE TABLE! HONEY?
LISTEN TO YOUR MOTHER.
SHE'D EAT IF WE WERE HAVING TONY-LOAF.
THAT'S IT!
AAARGH!
UMMFH!
YOU STARTED IT!
OW! NO FORCE FIELDS!

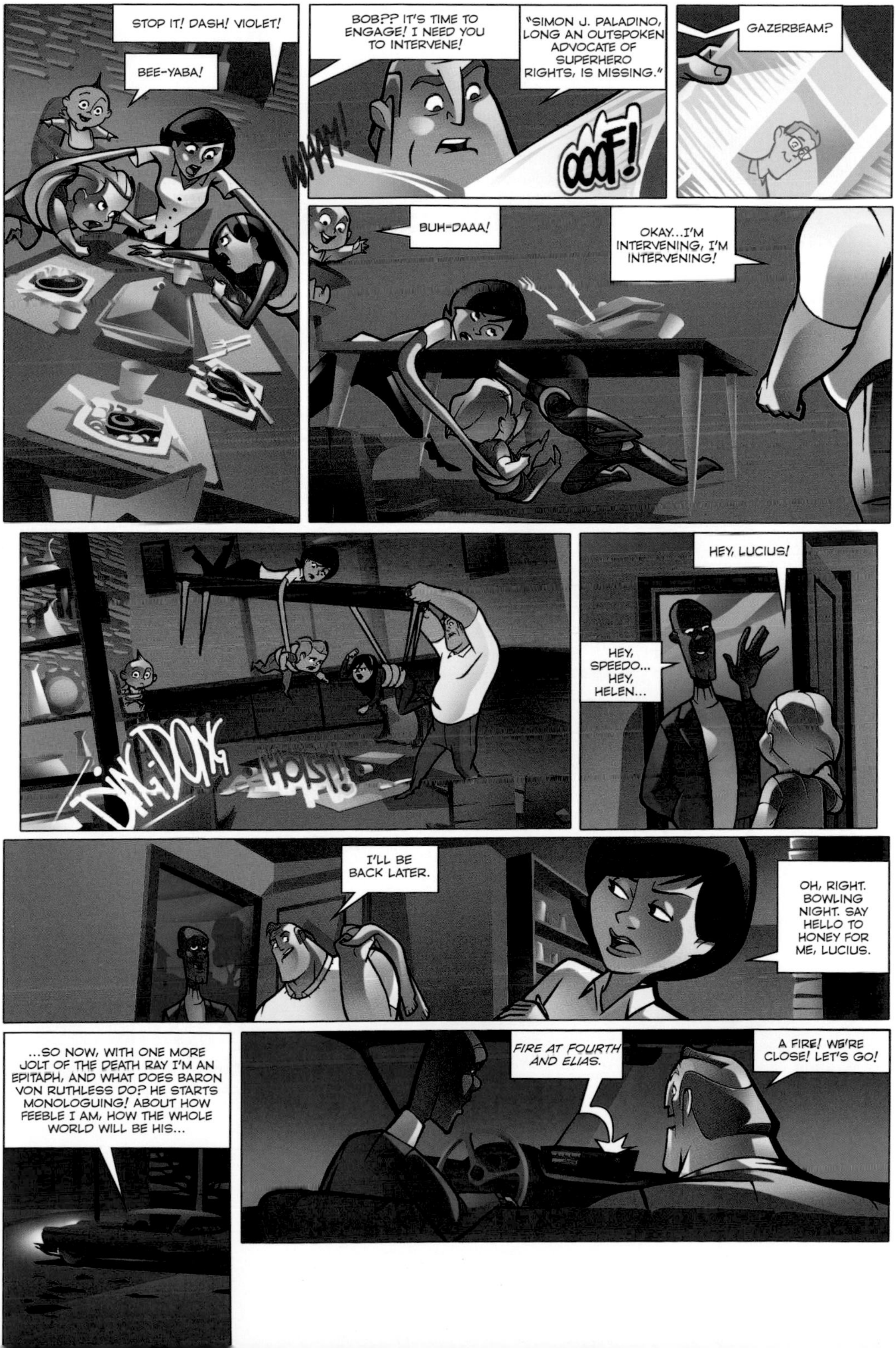
STOP IT! DASH! VIOLET!
BEE-YABA!
WHAM!
BOB?? IT'S TIME TO ENGAGE! I NEED YOU TO INTERVENE!
"SIMON J. PALADINO, LONG AN OUTSPOKEN ADVOCATE OF SUPERHERO RIGHTS, IS MISSING."
OOOF!
GAZERBEAM?
BUH-DAAA!
OKAY...I'M INTERVENING, I'M INTERVENING!
DING-DONG
HOIST!
HEY, LUCIUS!
HEY, SPEEDO... HEY, HELEN...
I'LL BE BACK LATER.
OH, RIGHT. BOWLING NIGHT. SAY HELLO TO HONEY FOR ME, LUCIUS.
...SO NOW, WITH ONE MORE JOLT OF THE DEATH RAY I'M AN EPITAPH, AND WHAT DOES BARON VON RUTHLESS DO? HE STARTS MONOLOGUING! ABOUT HOW FEEBLE I AM, HOW THE WHOLE WORLD WILL BE HIS...
FIRE AT FOURTH AND ELIAS.
A FIRE! WE'RE CLOSE! LET'S GO!

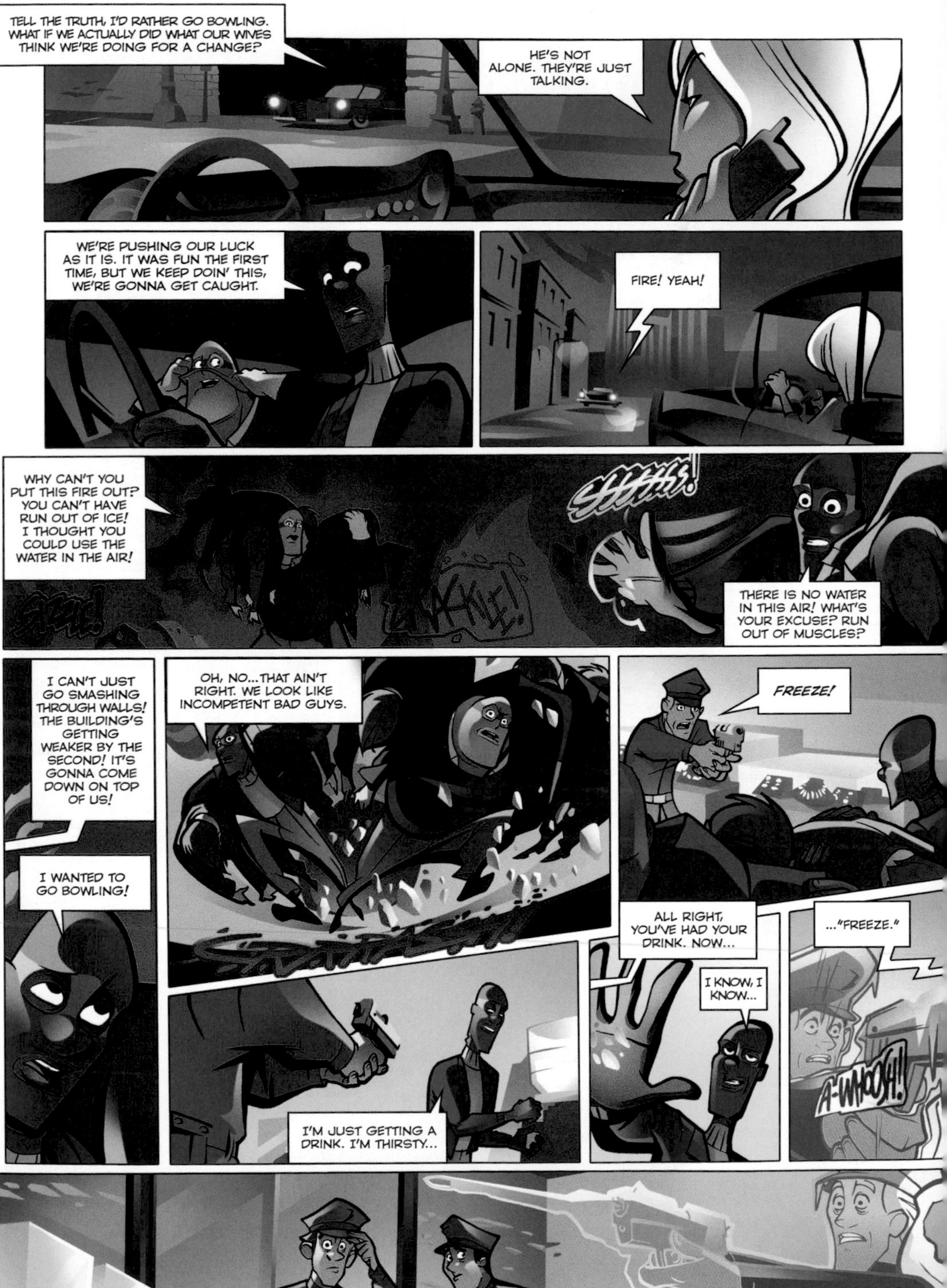
TELL THE TRUTH, I'D RATHER GO BOWLING. WHAT IF WE ACTUALLY DID WHAT OUR WIVES THINK WE'RE DOING FOR A CHANGE?
HE'S NOT ALONE. THEY'RE JUST TALKING.
WE'RE PUSHING OUR LUCK AS IT IS. IT WAS FUN THE FIRST TIME, BUT WE KEEP DOIN' THIS, WE'RE GONNA GET CAUGHT.
FIRE! YEAH!
WHY CAN'T YOU PUT THIS FIRE OUT? YOU CAN'T HAVE RUN OUT OF ICE! I THOUGHT YOU COULD USE THE WATER IN THE AIR!
THERE IS NO WATER IN THIS AIR! WHAT'S YOUR EXCUSE? RUN OUT OF MUSCLES?
I CAN'T JUST GO SMASHING THROUGH WALLS! THE BUILDING'S GETTING WEAKER BY THE SECOND! IT'S GONNA COME DOWN ON TOP OF US!
I WANTED TO GO BOWLING!
OH, NO...THAT AIN'T RIGHT. WE LOOK LIKE INCOMPETENT BAD GUYS.
FREEZE!
I'M JUST GETTING A DRINK. I'M THIRSTY...
ALL RIGHT, YOU'VE HAD YOUR DRINK. NOW...
I KNOW, I KNOW...
..."FREEZE."
A-WHOOSH!!

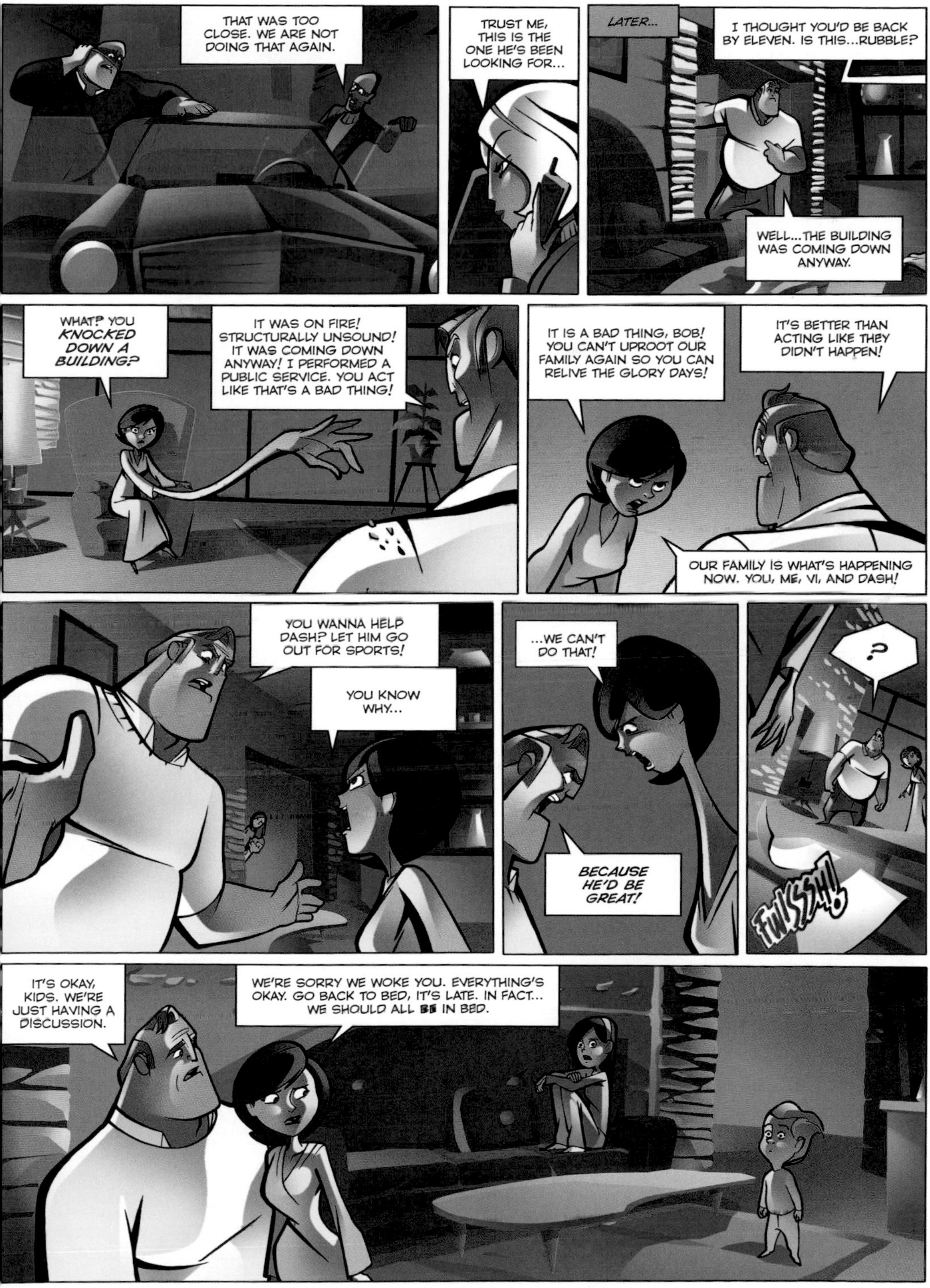
THAT WAS TOO CLOSE. WE ARE NOT DOING THAT AGAIN.
TRUST ME, THIS IS THE ONE HE'S BEEN LOOKING FOR...
LATER...
I THOUGHT YOU'D BE BACK BY ELEVEN. IS THIS...RUBBLE?
WELL...THE BUILDING WAS COMING DOWN ANYWAY.
WHAT? YOU *KNOCKED DOWN A BUILDING?*
IT WAS ON FIRE! STRUCTURALLY UNSOUND! IT WAS COMING DOWN ANYWAY! I PERFORMED A PUBLIC SERVICE. YOU ACT LIKE THAT'S A BAD THING!
IT IS A BAD THING, BOB! YOU CAN'T UPROOT OUR FAMILY AGAIN SO YOU CAN RELIVE THE GLORY DAYS!
IT'S BETTER THAN ACTING LIKE THEY DIDN'T HAPPEN!
OUR FAMILY IS WHAT'S HAPPENING NOW. YOU, ME, VI, AND DASH!
YOU WANNA HELP DASH? LET HIM GO OUT FOR SPORTS!
YOU KNOW WHY...
...WE CAN'T DO THAT!
BECAUSE HE'D BE GREAT!
?
FWUSSSH!
IT'S OKAY, KIDS. WE'RE JUST HAVING A DISCUSSION.
WE'RE SORRY WE WOKE YOU. EVERYTHING'S OKAY. GO BACK TO BED, IT'S LATE. IN FACT... WE SHOULD ALL BE IN BED.

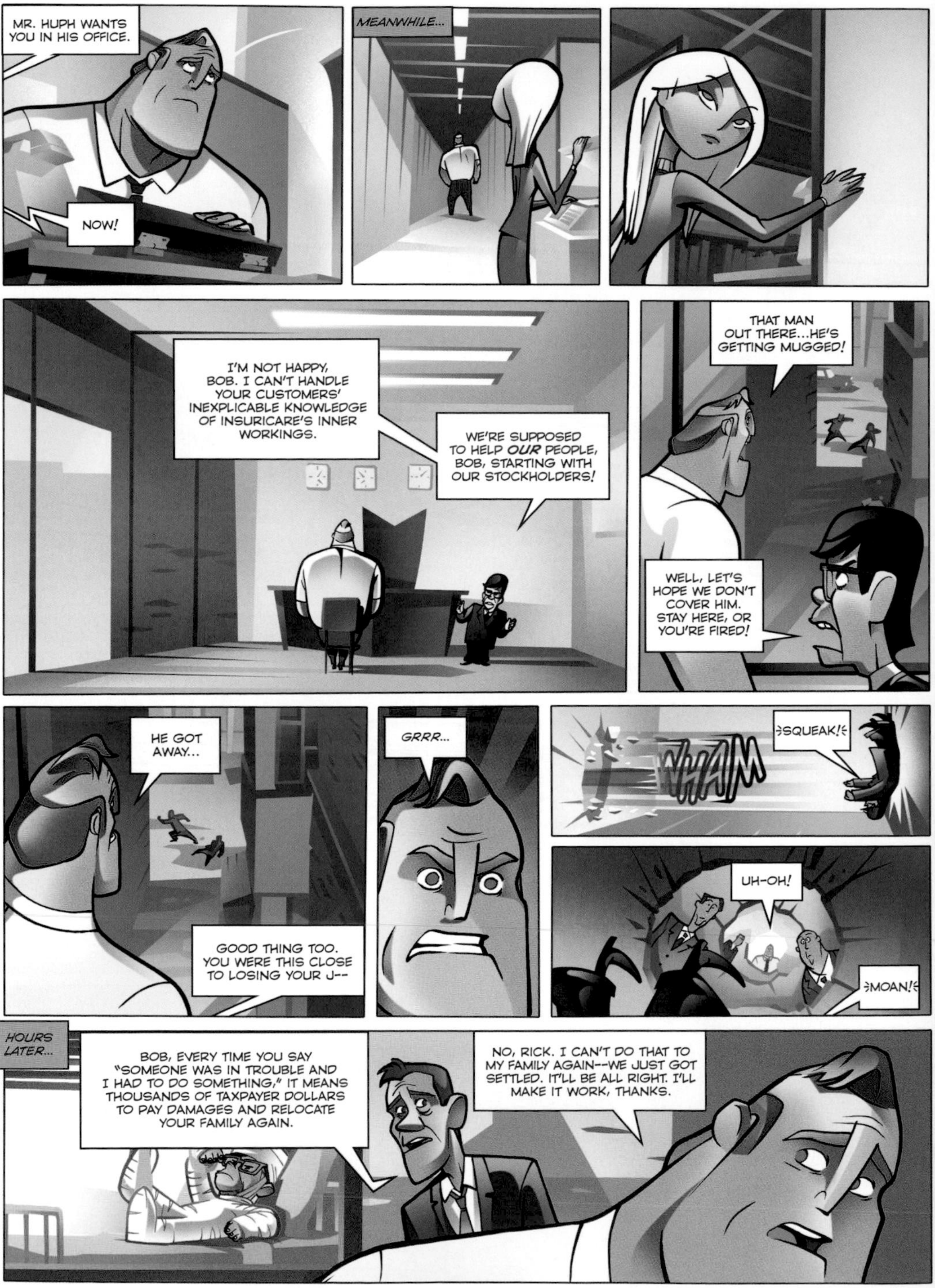
MR. HUPH WANTS YOU IN HIS OFFICE.
NOW!
MEANWHILE...
I'M NOT HAPPY, BOB. I CAN'T HANDLE YOUR CUSTOMERS' INEXPLICABLE KNOWLEDGE OF INSURICARE'S INNER WORKINGS.
WE'RE SUPPOSED TO HELP *OUR* PEOPLE, BOB, STARTING WITH OUR STOCKHOLDERS!
THAT MAN OUT THERE...HE'S GETTING MUGGED!
WELL, LET'S HOPE WE DON'T COVER HIM. STAY HERE, OR YOU'RE FIRED!
HE GOT AWAY...
GOOD THING TOO. YOU WERE THIS CLOSE TO LOSING YOUR J--
GRRR...
WHAM
SQUEAK!
UH-OH!
MOAN!
HOURS LATER...
BOB, EVERY TIME YOU SAY "SOMEONE WAS IN TROUBLE AND I HAD TO DO SOMETHING," IT MEANS THOUSANDS OF TAXPAYER DOLLARS TO PAY DAMAGES AND RELOCATE YOUR FAMILY AGAIN.
NO, RICK. I CAN'T DO THAT TO MY FAMILY AGAIN--WE JUST GOT SETTLED. IT'LL BE ALL RIGHT. I'LL MAKE IT WORK, THANKS.

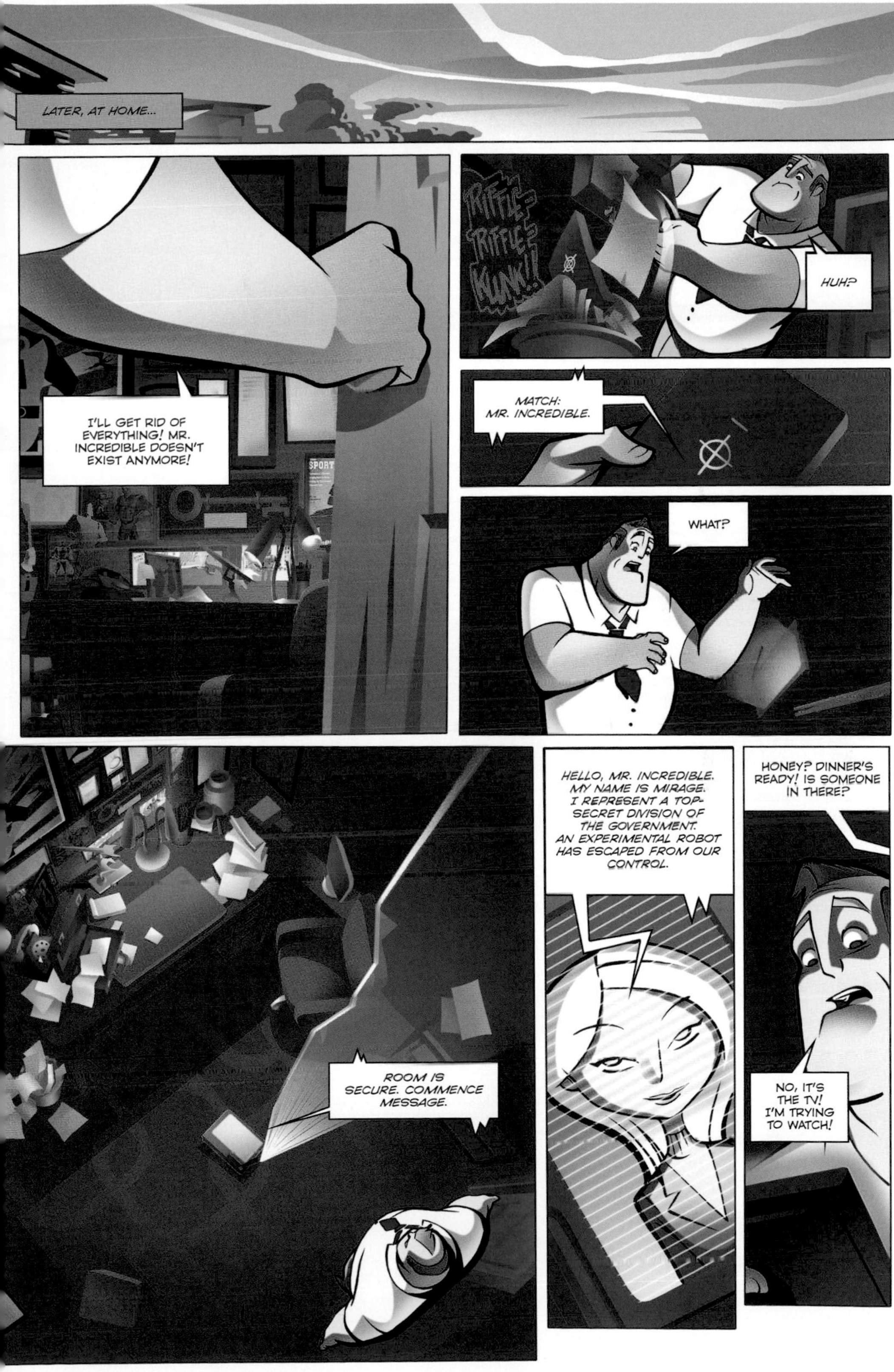
LATER, AT HOME...
I'LL GET RID OF EVERYTHING! MR. INCREDIBLE DOESN'T EXIST ANYMORE!
RIFFLE! RIFFLE! KLUNK!!
HUH?
MATCH: MR. INCREDIBLE.
WHAT?
ROOM IS SECURE. COMMENCE MESSAGE.
HELLO, MR. INCREDIBLE. MY NAME IS MIRAGE. I REPRESENT A TOP-SECRET DIVISION OF THE GOVERNMENT. AN EXPERIMENTAL ROBOT HAS ESCAPED FROM OUR CONTROL.
HONEY? DINNER'S READY! IS SOMEONE IN THERE?
NO, IT'S THE TV! I'M TRYING TO WATCH!

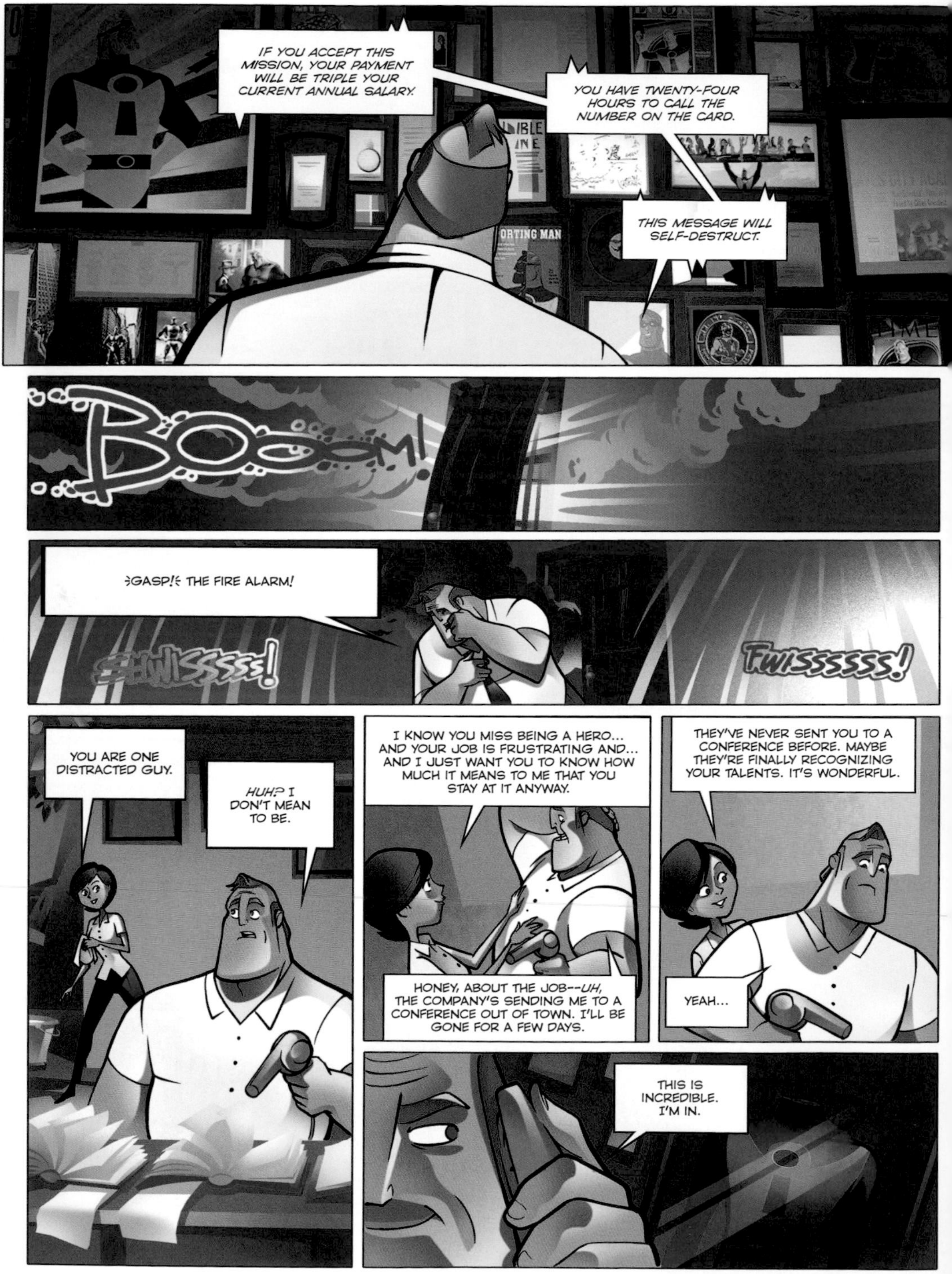
IF YOU ACCEPT THIS MISSION, YOUR PAYMENT WILL BE TRIPLE YOUR CURRENT ANNUAL SALARY.
YOU HAVE TWENTY-FOUR HOURS TO CALL THE NUMBER ON THE CARD.
THIS MESSAGE WILL SELF-DESTRUCT.
BOOOOM!
GASP! THE FIRE ALARM!
FWISSSSSS!
YOU ARE ONE DISTRACTED GUY.
HUH? I DON'T MEAN TO BE.
I KNOW YOU MISS BEING A HERO... AND YOUR JOB IS FRUSTRATING AND... AND I JUST WANT YOU TO KNOW HOW MUCH IT MEANS TO ME THAT YOU STAY AT IT ANYWAY.
HONEY, ABOUT THE JOB--UH, THE COMPANY'S SENDING ME TO A CONFERENCE OUT OF TOWN. I'LL BE GONE FOR A FEW DAYS.
THEY'VE NEVER SENT YOU TO A CONFERENCE BEFORE. MAYBE THEY'RE FINALLY RECOGNIZING YOUR TALENTS. IT'S WONDERFUL.
YEAH...
THIS IS INCREDIBLE. I'M IN.

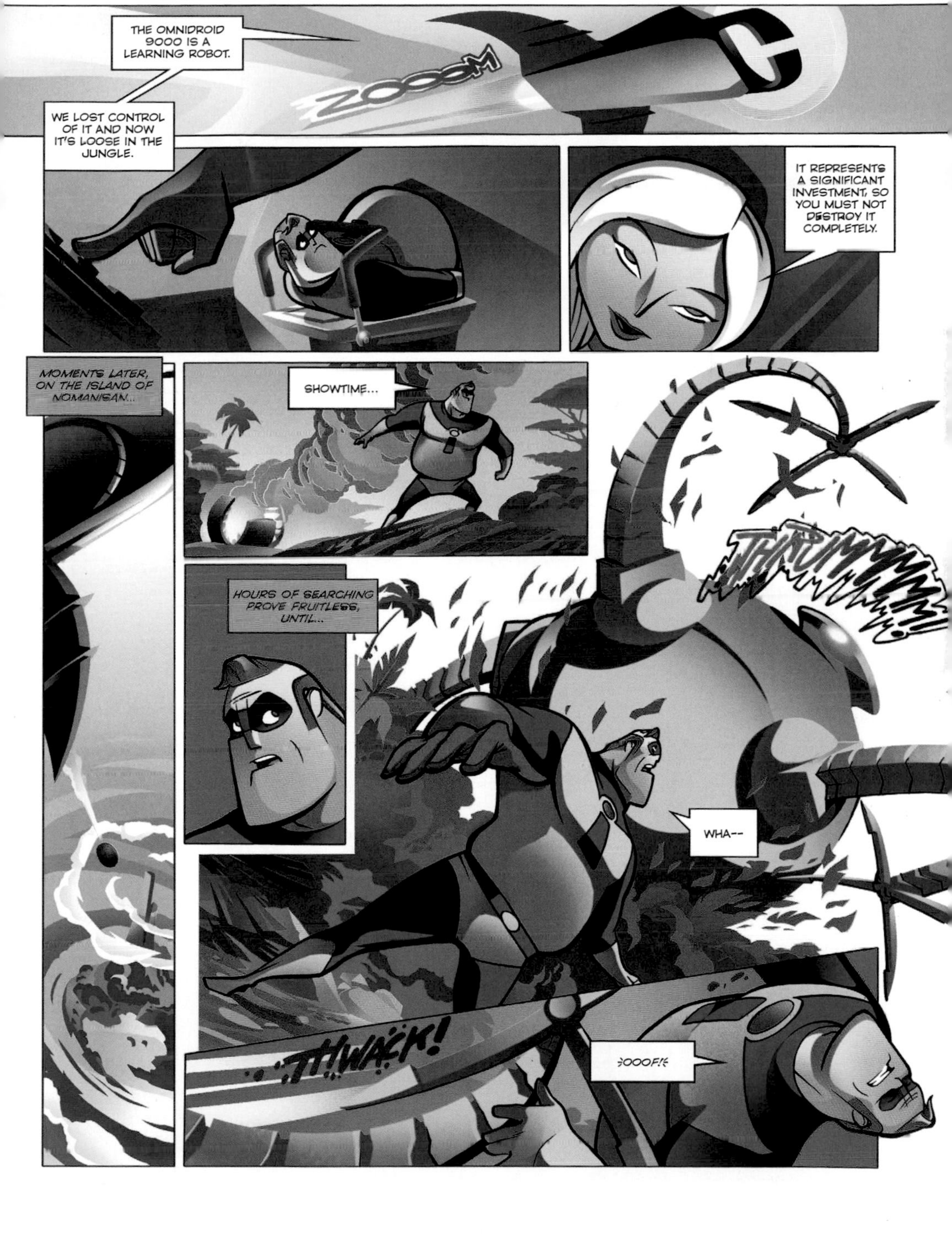
THE OMNIDROID 9000 IS A LEARNING ROBOT.
ZOOOOM
WE LOST CONTROL OF IT AND NOW IT'S LOOSE IN THE JUNGLE.
IT REPRESENTS A SIGNIFICANT INVESTMENT, SO YOU MUST NOT DESTROY IT COMPLETELY.
MOMENTS LATER, ON THE ISLAND OF NOMANISAN...
SHOWTIME...
HOURS OF SEARCHING PROVE FRUITLESS, UNTIL...
THRUMMMM!!
WHA--
THWACK!
OOOF!

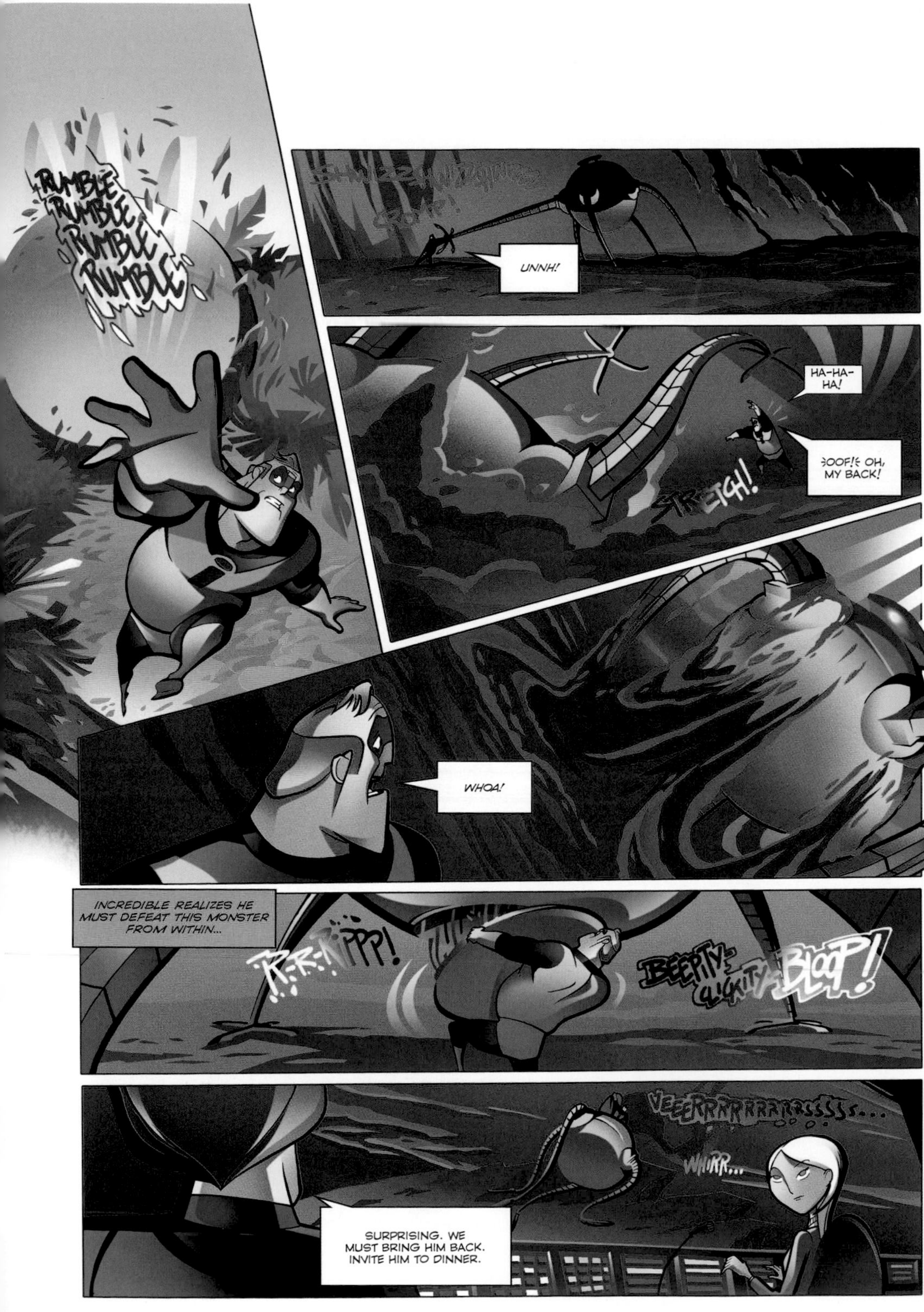
RUMBLE RUMBLE RUMBLE RUMBLE
UNNH!
HA-HA-HA!
OOF! OH, MY BACK!
STRETCH!
WHOA!
INCREDIBLE REALIZES HE MUST DEFEAT THIS MONSTER FROM WITHIN...
R-R-RIPPP!
BEEPITY-CLICKITY-BLOOP!
VEEERRRRRRRRRRSSSSS...
WHIRR...
SURPRISING. WE MUST BRING HIM BACK. INVITE HIM TO DINNER.

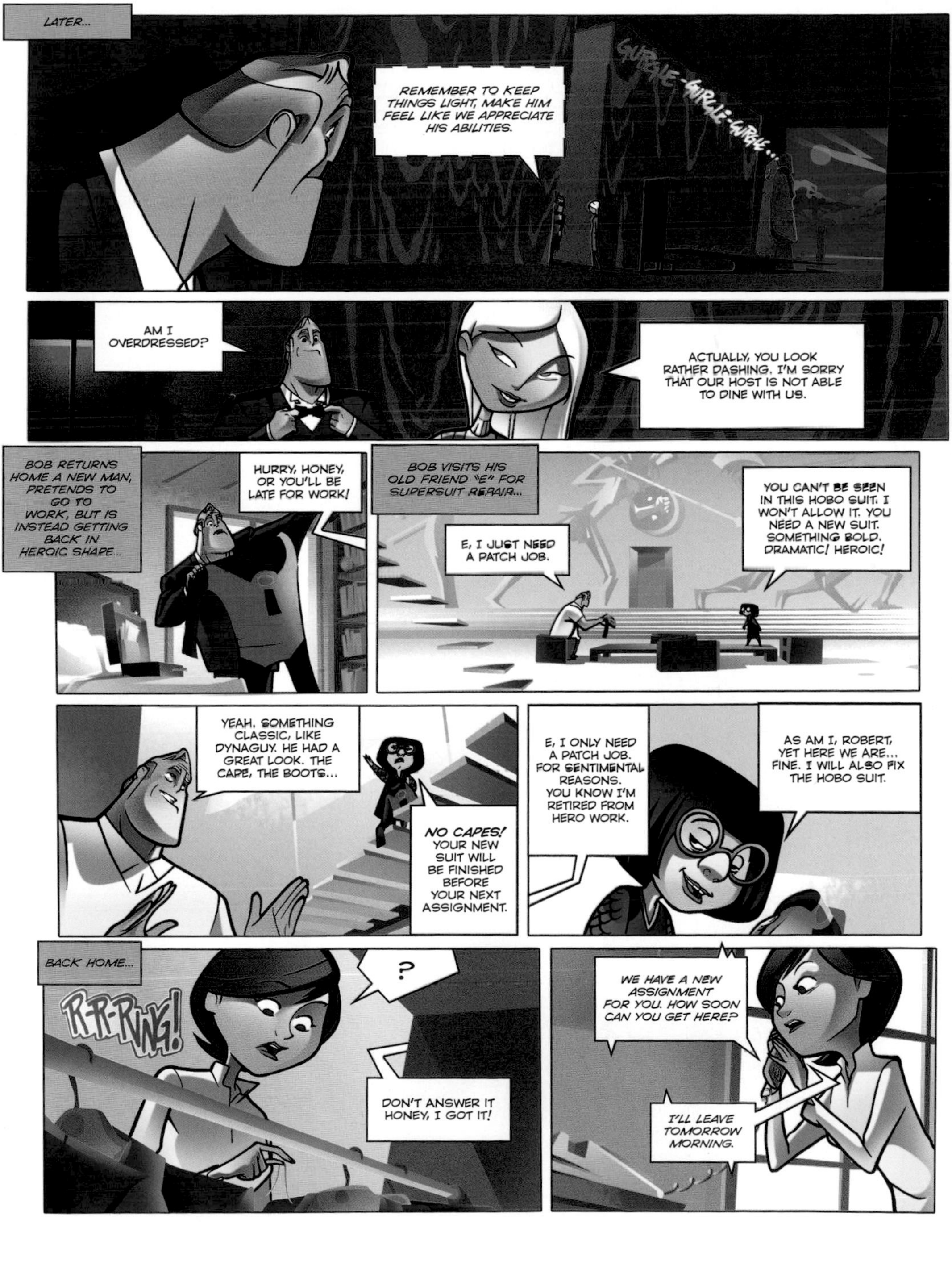
LATER...
REMEMBER TO KEEP THINGS LIGHT, MAKE HIM FEEL LIKE WE APPRECIATE HIS ABILITIES.
GURGLE-GURGLE-GURGLE...
AM I OVERDRESSED?
ACTUALLY, YOU LOOK RATHER DASHING. I'M SORRY THAT OUR HOST IS NOT ABLE TO DINE WITH US.
BOB RETURNS HOME A NEW MAN, PRETENDS TO GO TO WORK, BUT IS INSTEAD GETTING BACK IN HEROIC SHAPE...
HURRY, HONEY, OR YOU'LL BE LATE FOR WORK!
BOB VISITS HIS OLD FRIEND "E" FOR SUPERSUIT REPAIR...
E, I JUST NEED A PATCH JOB.
YOU CAN'T BE SEEN IN THIS HOBO SUIT. I WON'T ALLOW IT. YOU NEED A NEW SUIT. SOMETHING BOLD. DRAMATIC! HEROIC!
YEAH. SOMETHING CLASSIC, LIKE DYNAGUY. HE HAD A GREAT LOOK. THE CAPE, THE BOOTS...
NO CAPES! YOUR NEW SUIT WILL BE FINISHED BEFORE YOUR NEXT ASSIGNMENT.
E, I ONLY NEED A PATCH JOB. FOR SENTIMENTAL REASONS. YOU KNOW I'M RETIRED FROM HERO WORK.
AS AM I, ROBERT, YET HERE WE ARE... FINE. I WILL ALSO FIX THE HOBO SUIT.
BACK HOME...
R-R-RING!
?
DON'T ANSWER IT HONEY, I GOT IT!
WE HAVE A NEW ASSIGNMENT FOR YOU. HOW SOON CAN YOU GET HERE?
I'LL LEAVE TOMORROW MORNING.

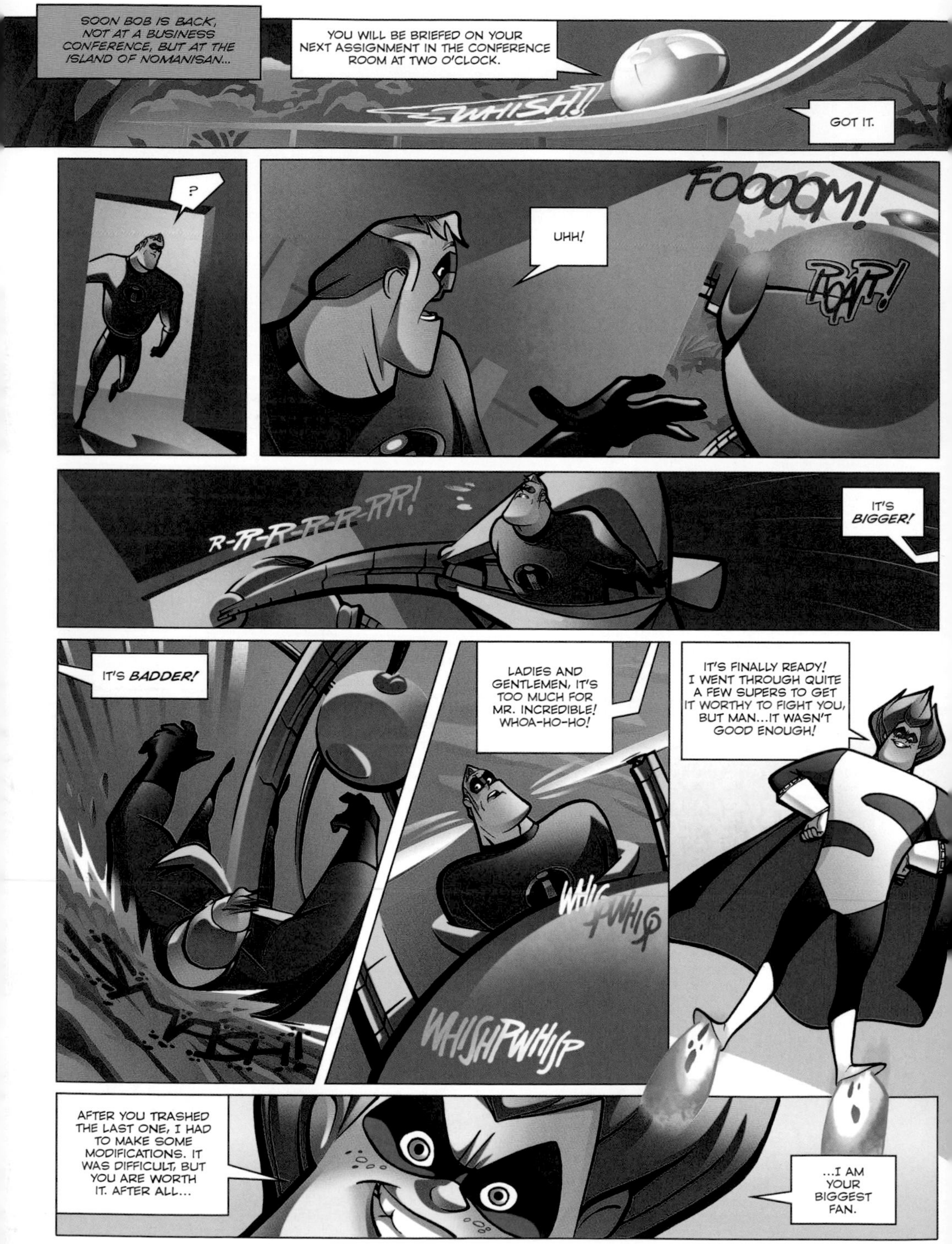
SOON BOB IS BACK, NOT AT A BUSINESS CONFERENCE, BUT AT THE ISLAND OF NOMANISAN...
YOU WILL BE BRIEFED ON YOUR NEXT ASSIGNMENT IN THE CONFERENCE ROOM AT TWO O'CLOCK.
WHISH!
GOT IT.
?
FOOOOM!
UHH!
R-R-R-R-R-RR!
IT'S BIGGER!
IT'S BADDER!
LADIES AND GENTLEMEN, IT'S TOO MUCH FOR MR. INCREDIBLE! WHOA-HO-HO!
IT'S FINALLY READY! I WENT THROUGH QUITE A FEW SUPERS TO GET IT WORTHY TO FIGHT YOU, BUT MAN...IT WASN'T GOOD ENOUGH!
WHISHPWHISP
AFTER YOU TRASHED THE LAST ONE, I HAD TO MAKE SOME MODIFICATIONS. IT WAS DIFFICULT, BUT YOU ARE WORTH IT. AFTER ALL...
...I AM YOUR BIGGEST FAN.

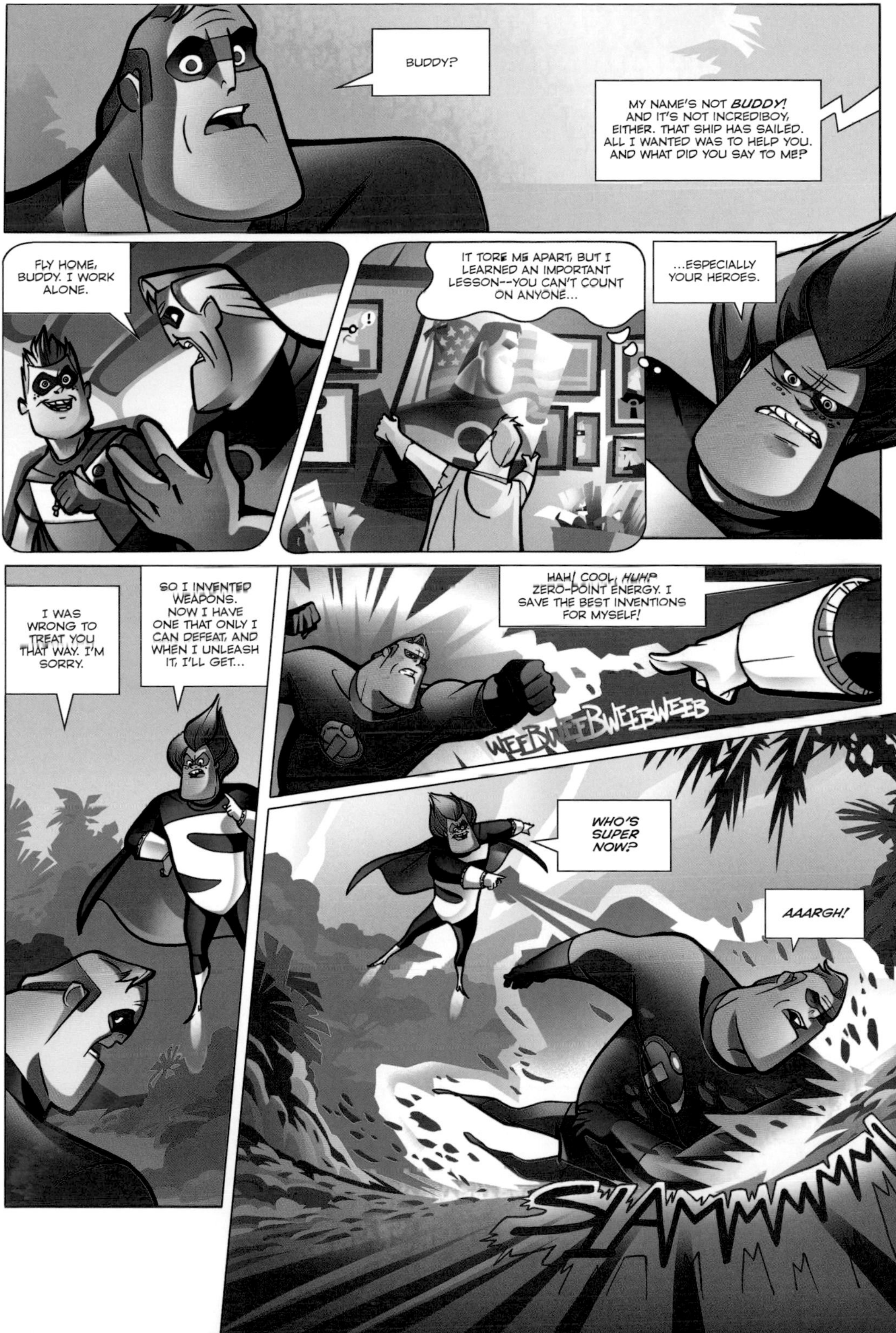
BUDDY?
MY NAME'S NOT *BUDDY!* AND IT'S NOT INCREDIBOY, EITHER. THAT SHIP HAS SAILED. ALL I WANTED WAS TO HELP YOU. AND WHAT DID YOU SAY TO ME?
FLY HOME, BUDDY. I WORK ALONE.
IT TORE ME APART, BUT I LEARNED AN IMPORTANT LESSON--YOU CAN'T COUNT ON ANYONE...
...ESPECIALLY YOUR HEROES.
I WAS WRONG TO TREAT YOU THAT WAY. I'M SORRY.
SO I INVENTED WEAPONS. NOW I HAVE ONE THAT ONLY I CAN DEFEAT, AND WHEN I UNLEASH IT, I'LL GET...
HAH! COOL, *HUH?* ZERO-POINT ENERGY. I SAVE THE BEST INVENTIONS FOR MYSELF!
WEEBWEEBWEEBWEEB
WHO'S SUPER NOW?
AAARGH!
SLAMMMM!

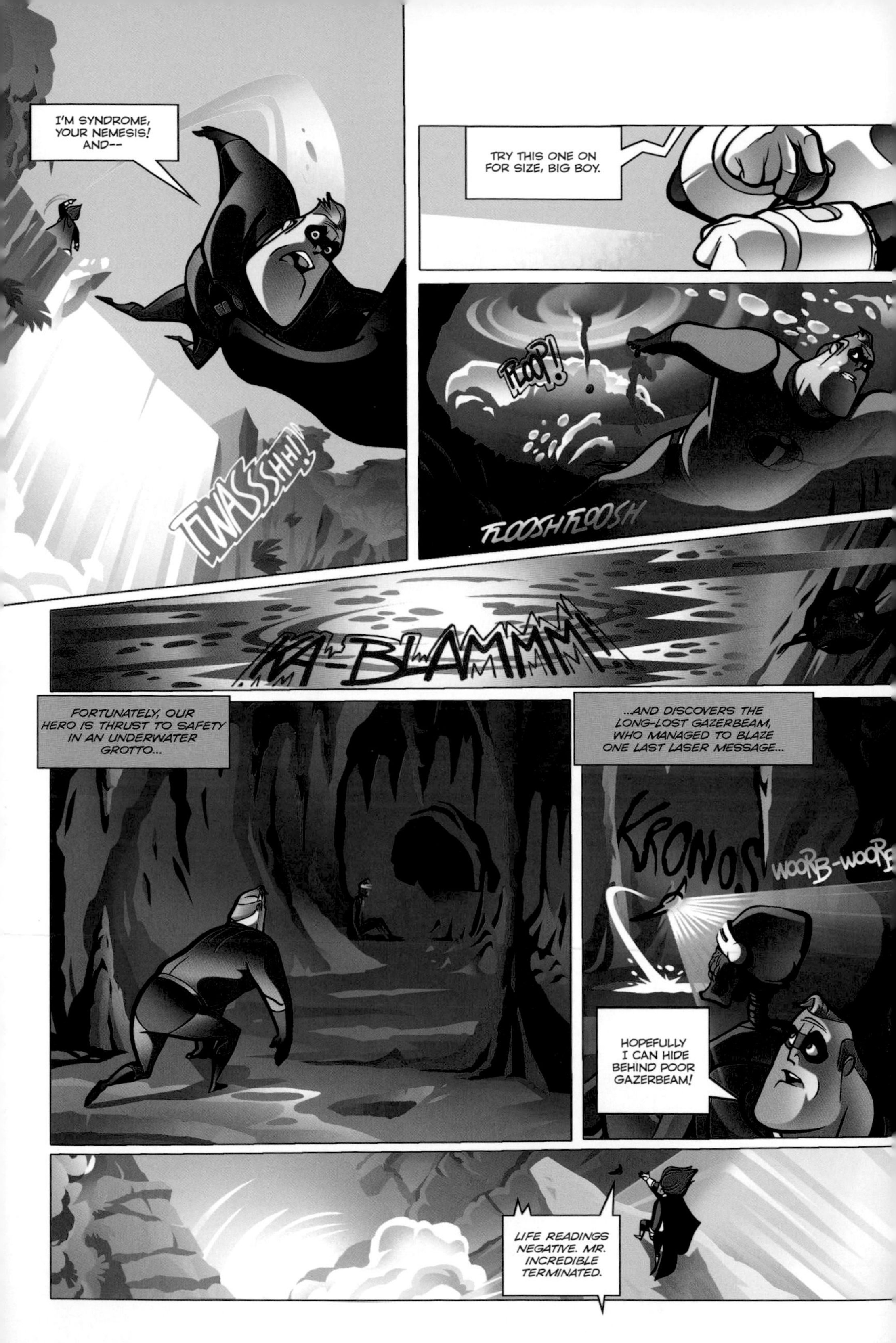
I'M SYNDROME, YOUR NEMESIS! AND--
FWASSSHH!
TRY THIS ONE ON FOR SIZE, BIG BOY.
FLOOP!
FLOOSHFLOOSH
KA-BLAMMM!
FORTUNATELY, OUR HERO IS THRUST TO SAFETY IN AN UNDERWATER GROTTO...
...AND DISCOVERS THE LONG-LOST GAZERBEAM, WHO MANAGED TO BLAZE ONE LAST LASER MESSAGE...
KRONOS
HOPEFULLY I CAN HIDE BEHIND POOR GAZERBEAM!
LIFE READINGS NEGATIVE. MR. INCREDIBLE TERMINATED.

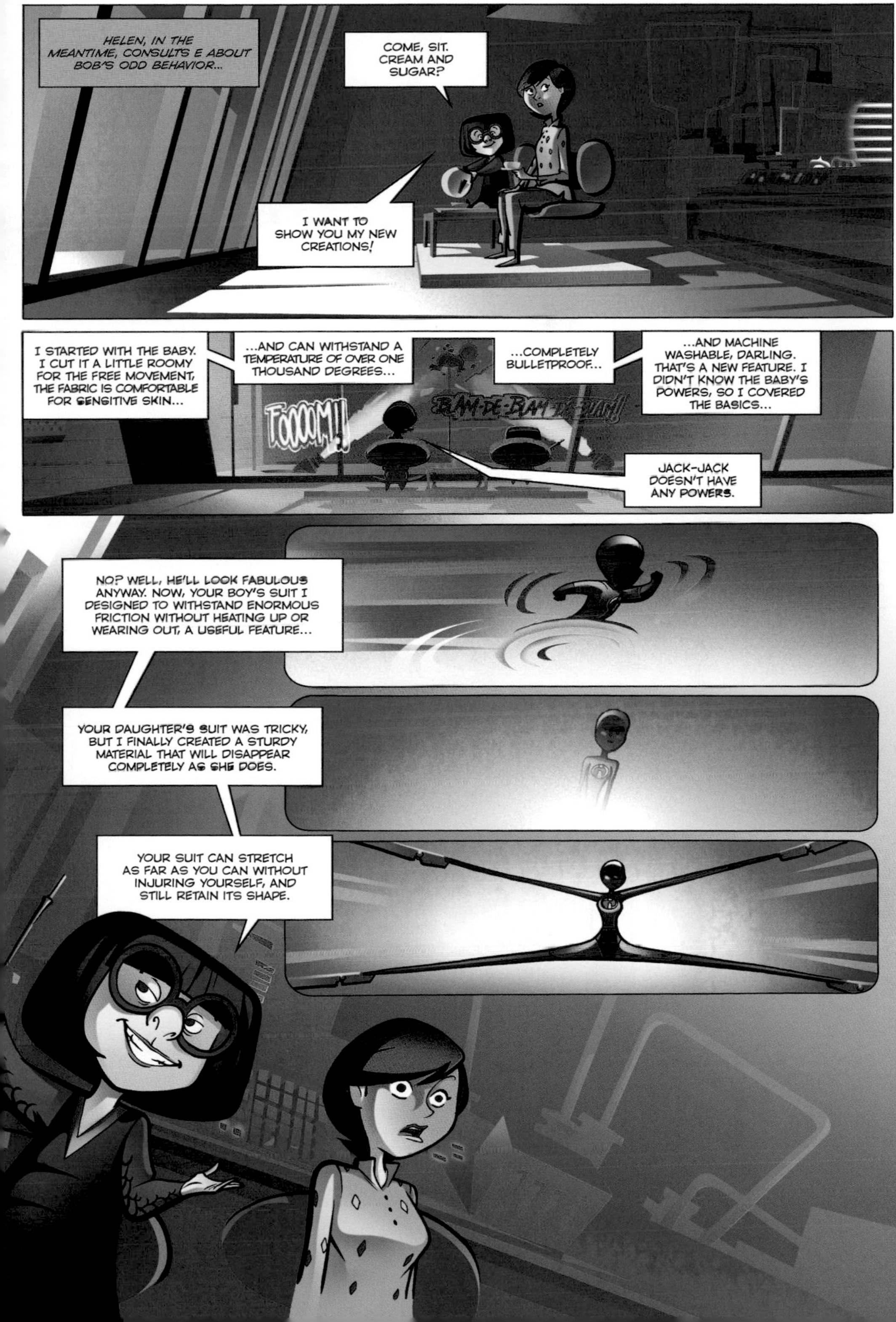
HELEN, IN THE MEANTIME, CONSULTS E ABOUT BOB'S ODD BEHAVIOR...
COME, SIT. CREAM AND SUGAR?
I WANT TO SHOW YOU MY NEW CREATIONS!
I STARTED WITH THE BABY. I CUT IT A LITTLE ROOMY FOR THE FREE MOVEMENT, THE FABRIC IS COMFORTABLE FOR SENSITIVE SKIN...
...AND CAN WITHSTAND A TEMPERATURE OF OVER ONE THOUSAND DEGREES...
FOOOOM!!
...COMPLETELY BULLETPROOF...
BLAM-DE-BLAM-DE-BLAM!
...AND MACHINE WASHABLE, DARLING. THAT'S A NEW FEATURE. I DIDN'T KNOW THE BABY'S POWERS, SO I COVERED THE BASICS...
JACK-JACK DOESN'T HAVE ANY POWERS.
NO? WELL, HE'LL LOOK FABULOUS ANYWAY. NOW, YOUR BOY'S SUIT I DESIGNED TO WITHSTAND ENORMOUS FRICTION WITHOUT HEATING UP OR WEARING OUT, A USEFUL FEATURE...
YOUR DAUGHTER'S SUIT WAS TRICKY, BUT I FINALLY CREATED A STURDY MATERIAL THAT WILL DISAPPEAR COMPLETELY AS SHE DOES.
YOUR SUIT CAN STRETCH AS FAR AS YOU CAN WITHOUT INJURING YOURSELF, AND STILL RETAIN ITS SHAPE.

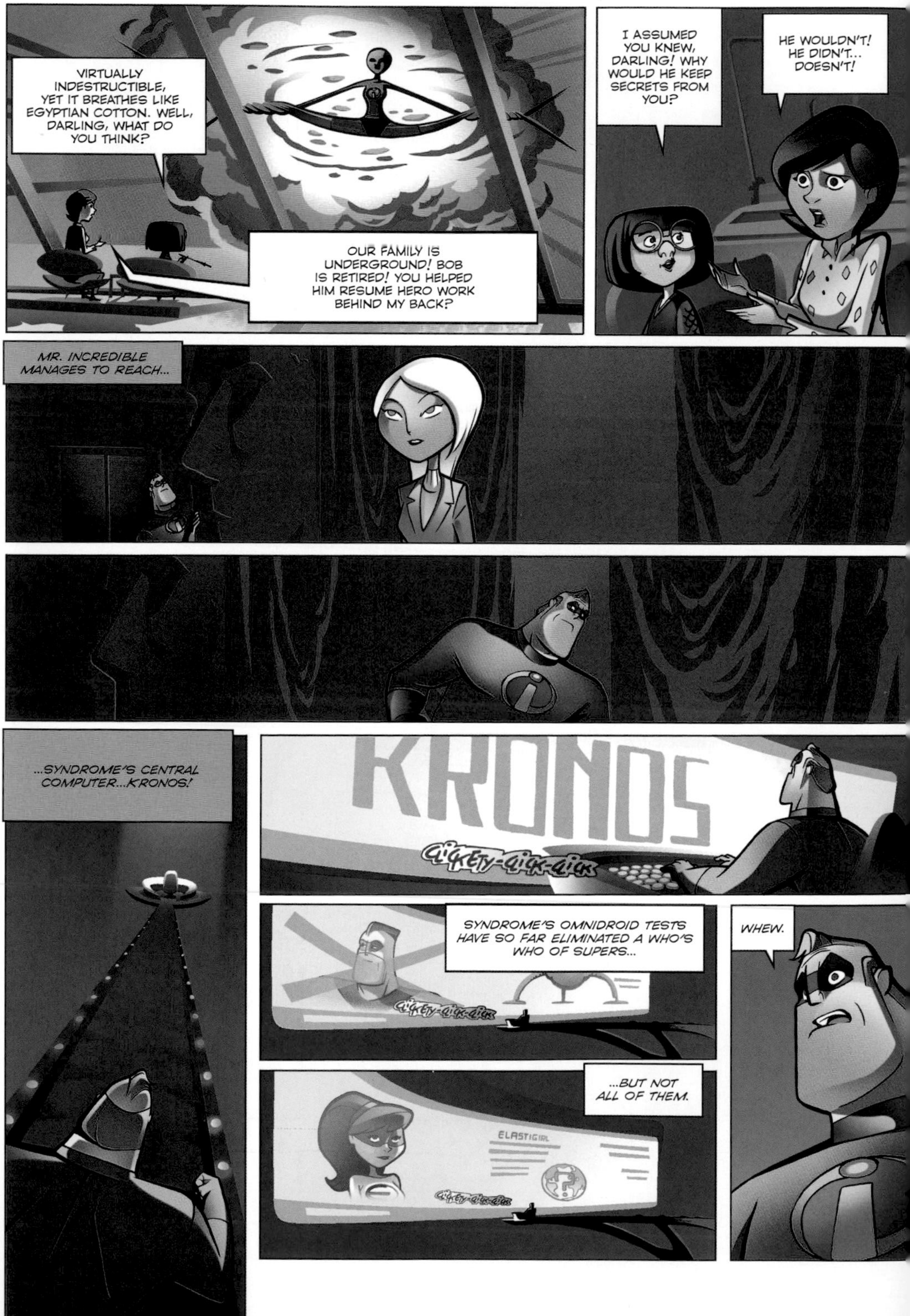
VIRTUALLY INDESTRUCTIBLE, YET IT BREATHES LIKE EGYPTIAN COTTON. WELL, DARLING, WHAT DO YOU THINK?
OUR FAMILY IS UNDERGROUND! BOB IS RETIRED! YOU HELPED HIM RESUME HERO WORK BEHIND MY BACK?
I ASSUMED YOU KNEW, DARLING! WHY WOULD HE KEEP SECRETS FROM YOU?
HE WOULDN'T! HE DIDN'T... DOESN'T!
MR. INCREDIBLE MANAGES TO REACH...
...SYNDROME'S CENTRAL COMPUTER...KRONOS!
KRONOS
CLICKETY-CLICK-CLICK
SYNDROME'S OMNIDROID TESTS HAVE SO FAR ELIMINATED A WHO'S WHO OF SUPERS...
CLICKETY-CLICK-CLICK
WHEW.
...BUT NOT ALL OF THEM.
ELASTIGIRL

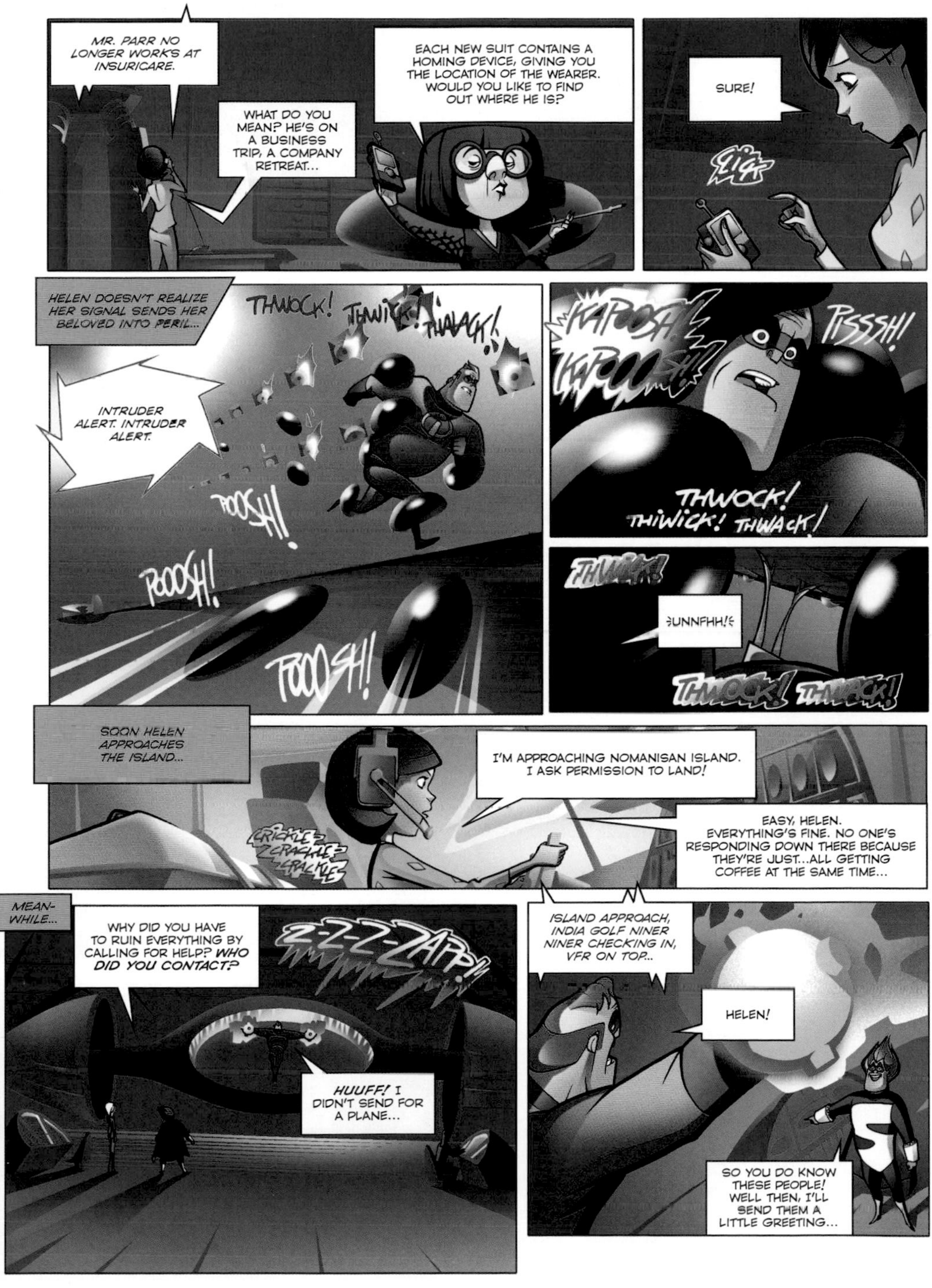
MR. PARR NO LONGER WORKS AT INSURICARE.
EACH NEW SUIT CONTAINS A HOMING DEVICE, GIVING YOU THE LOCATION OF THE WEARER. WOULD YOU LIKE TO FIND OUT WHERE HE IS?
WHAT DO YOU MEAN? HE'S ON A BUSINESS TRIP, A COMPANY RETREAT...
SURE!
CLICK
HELEN DOESN'T REALIZE HER SIGNAL SENDS HER BELOVED INTO PERIL...
THWOCK! THWICK! THWACK!
INTRUDER ALERT. INTRUDER ALERT.
POOSH!
POOOSH!
POOOSH!
KAPOOSH! KAPOOOSH!
PISSSH!
THWOCK! THIWICK! THWACK!
THWACK!
UNNFHH!
THWOCK! THWACK!
SOON HELEN APPROACHES THE ISLAND...
I'M APPROACHING NOMANISAN ISLAND. I ASK PERMISSION TO LAND!
CRICKLE CRACKLE CRACKLE
EASY, HELEN. EVERYTHING'S FINE. NO ONE'S RESPONDING DOWN THERE BECAUSE THEY'RE JUST...ALL GETTING COFFEE AT THE SAME TIME...
MEAN-WHILE...
WHY DID YOU HAVE TO RUIN EVERYTHING BY CALLING FOR HELP? WHO DID YOU CONTACT?
Z-Z-Z-ZAPP!
HUUFF! I DIDN'T SEND FOR A PLANE...
ISLAND APPROACH, INDIA GOLF NINER NINER CHECKING IN, VFR ON TOP...
HELEN!
SO YOU DO KNOW THESE PEOPLE! WELL THEN, I'LL SEND THEM A LITTLE GREETING...

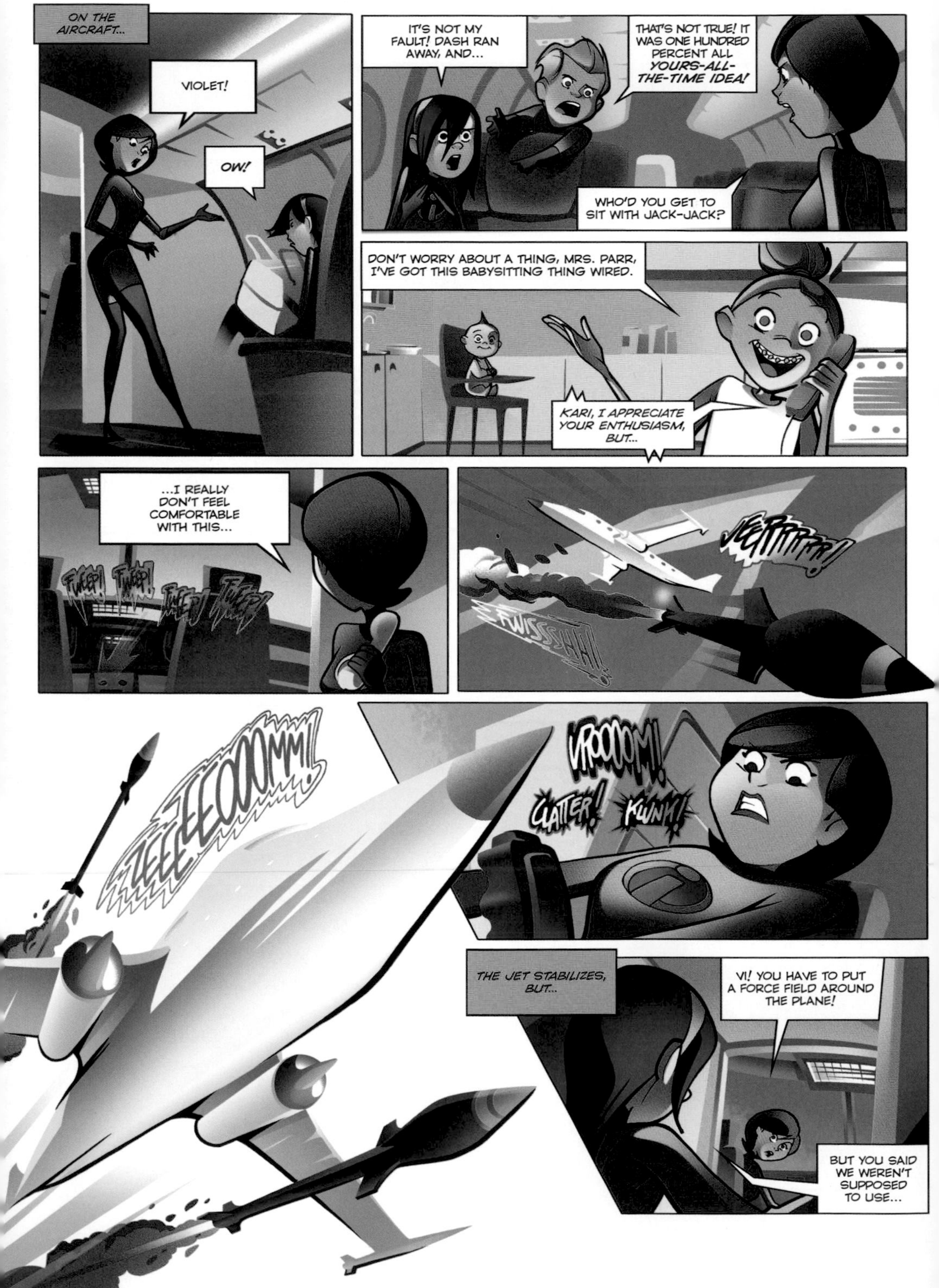

ON THE AIRCRAFT...
VIOLET!
OW!
IT'S NOT MY FAULT! DASH RAN AWAY, AND...
THAT'S NOT TRUE! IT WAS ONE HUNDRED PERCENT ALL YOURS-ALL-THE-TIME IDEA!
WHO'D YOU GET TO SIT WITH JACK-JACK?
DON'T WORRY ABOUT A THING, MRS. PARR, I'VE GOT THIS BABYSITTING THING WIRED.
KARI, I APPRECIATE YOUR ENTHUSIASM, BUT...
...I REALLY DON'T FEEL COMFORTABLE WITH THIS...
FWEEP! TWEEP! TWEEP! TWEEP!
VEERRRRR!
FWISSSHH!
ZEEEEEOOOMM!
VROOOOM!
CLATTER! KLUNK!
THE JET STABILIZES, BUT...
VI! YOU HAVE TO PUT A FORCE FIELD AROUND THE PLANE!
BUT YOU SAID WE WEREN'T SUPPOSED TO USE...

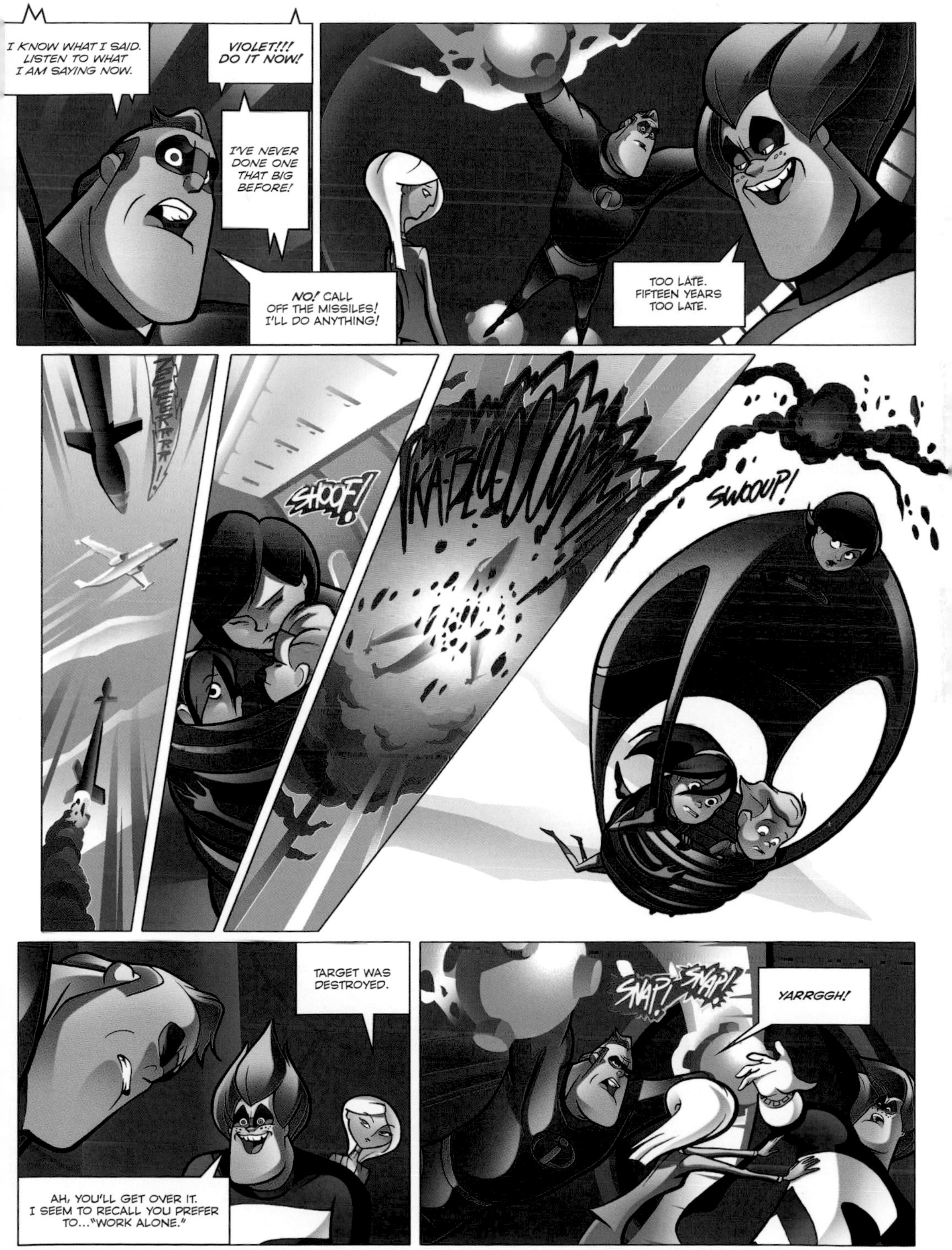
I KNOW WHAT I SAID. LISTEN TO WHAT I AM SAYING NOW.
VIOLET!!! DO IT NOW!
I'VE NEVER DONE ONE THAT BIG BEFORE!
NO! CALL OFF THE MISSILES! I'LL DO ANYTHING!
TOO LATE. FIFTEEN YEARS TOO LATE.
SHOOF!
SWOOUP!
TARGET WAS DESTROYED.
AH, YOU'LL GET OVER IT. I SEEM TO RECALL YOU PREFER TO..."WORK ALONE."
SNAP! SNAP!
YARRGGH!

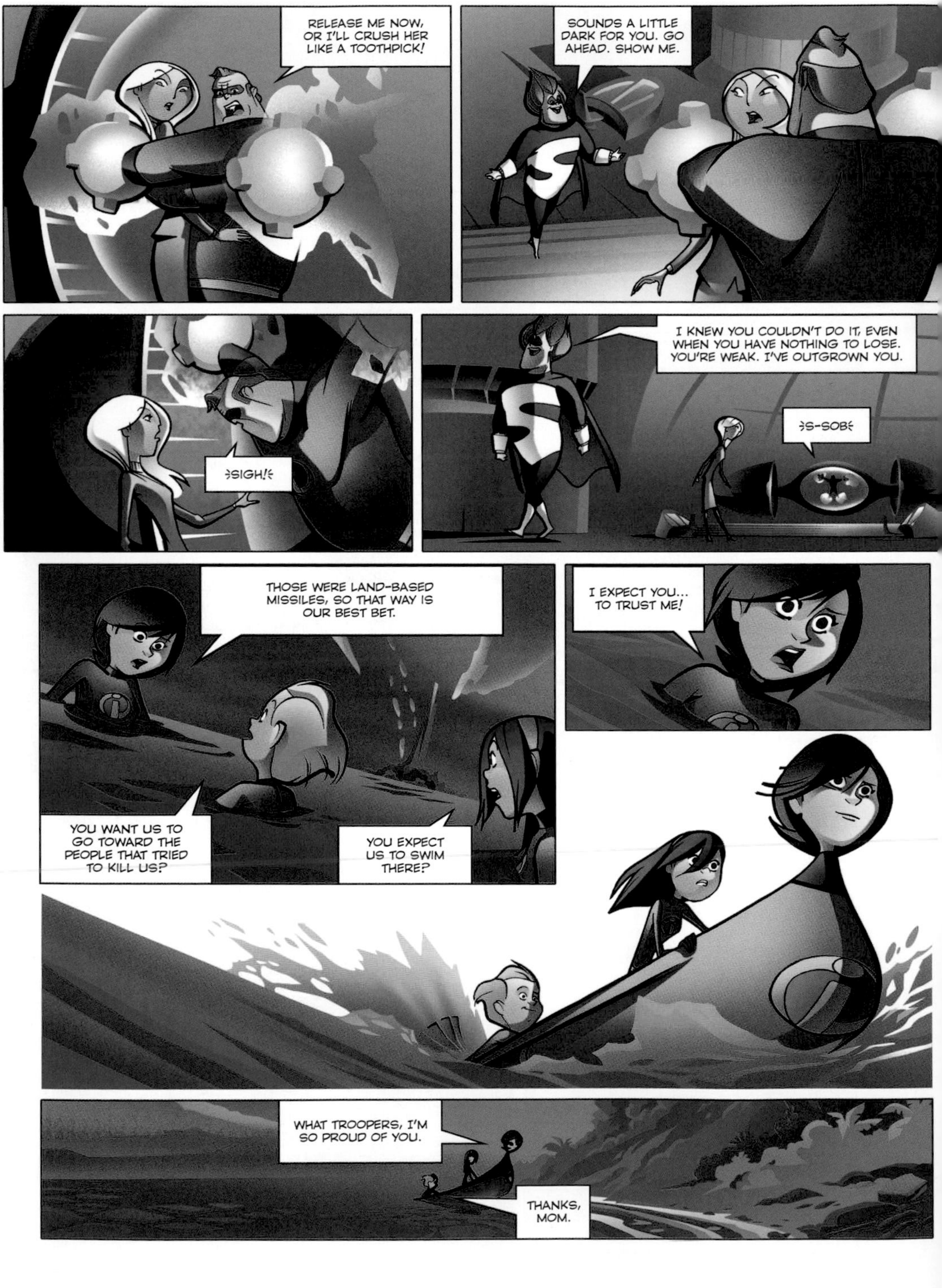
RELEASE ME NOW, OR I'LL CRUSH HER LIKE A TOOTHPICK!
SOUNDS A LITTLE DARK FOR YOU. GO AHEAD. SHOW ME.
SIGH!
I KNEW YOU COULDN'T DO IT, EVEN WHEN YOU HAVE NOTHING TO LOSE. YOU'RE WEAK. I'VE OUTGROWN YOU.
S-SOB
THOSE WERE LAND-BASED MISSILES, SO THAT WAY IS OUR BEST BET.
YOU WANT US TO GO TOWARD THE PEOPLE THAT TRIED TO KILL US?
YOU EXPECT US TO SWIM THERE?
I EXPECT YOU... TO TRUST ME!
WHAT TROOPERS, I'M SO PROUD OF YOU.
THANKS, MOM.

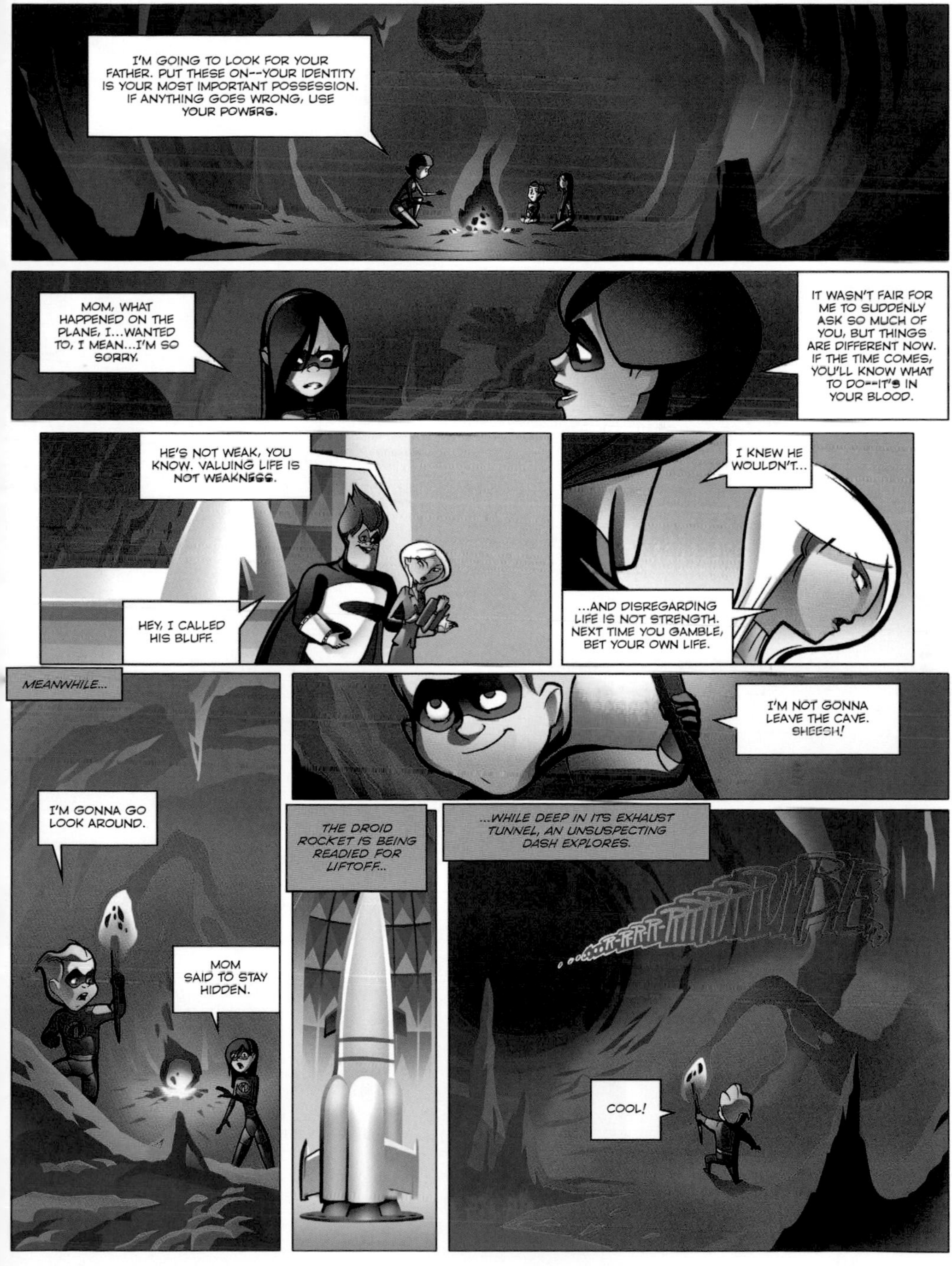
I'M GOING TO LOOK FOR YOUR FATHER. PUT THESE ON--YOUR IDENTITY IS YOUR MOST IMPORTANT POSSESSION. IF ANYTHING GOES WRONG, USE YOUR POWERS.
MOM, WHAT HAPPENED ON THE PLANE, I...WANTED TO, I MEAN...I'M SO SORRY.
IT WASN'T FAIR FOR ME TO SUDDENLY ASK SO MUCH OF YOU, BUT THINGS ARE DIFFERENT NOW. IF THE TIME COMES, YOU'LL KNOW WHAT TO DO--IT'S IN YOUR BLOOD.
HE'S NOT WEAK, YOU KNOW. VALUING LIFE IS NOT WEAKNESS.
HEY, I CALLED HIS BLUFF.
I KNEW HE WOULDN'T...
...AND DISREGARDING LIFE IS NOT STRENGTH. NEXT TIME YOU GAMBLE, BET YOUR OWN LIFE.
MEANWHILE...
I'M GONNA GO LOOK AROUND.
MOM SAID TO STAY HIDDEN.
I'M NOT GONNA LEAVE THE CAVE. SHEESH!
THE DROID ROCKET IS BEING READIED FOR LIFTOFF...
...WHILE DEEP IN ITS EXHAUST TUNNEL, AN UNSUSPECTING DASH EXPLORES.
COOL!

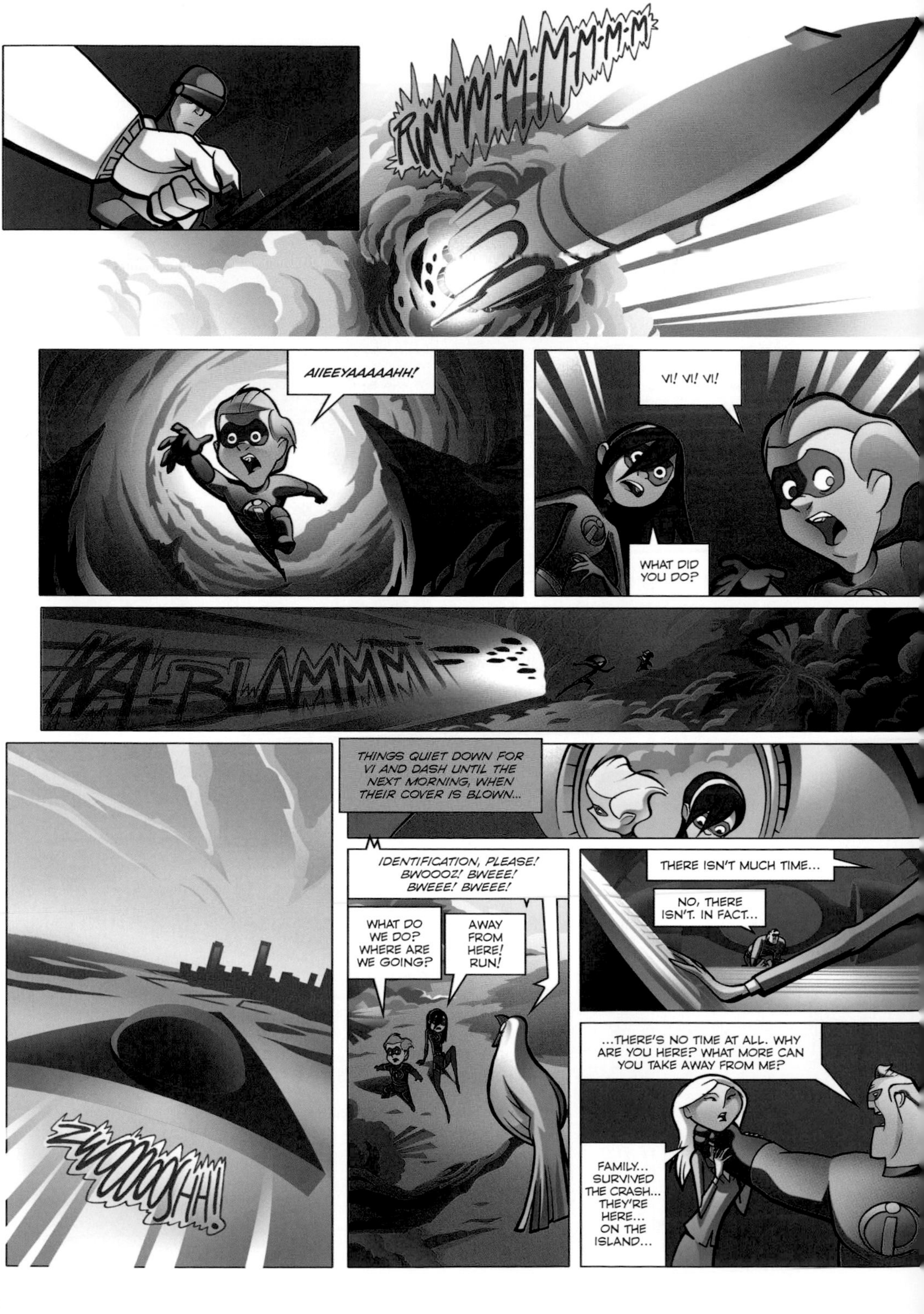
RUMMM-M-M-M-M-M
AIIEEYAAAAAAHH!
VI! VI! VI!
WHAT DID YOU DO?
KA-BLAMMM
THINGS QUIET DOWN FOR VI AND DASH UNTIL THE NEXT MORNING, WHEN THEIR COVER IS BLOWN...
ZWOOOOSHH!
IDENTIFICATION, PLEASE! BWOOOZ! BWEEE! BWEEE! BWEEE!
WHAT DO WE DO? WHERE ARE WE GOING?
AWAY FROM HERE! RUN!
THERE ISN'T MUCH TIME...
NO, THERE ISN'T. IN FACT...
...THERE'S NO TIME AT ALL. WHY ARE YOU HERE? WHAT MORE CAN YOU TAKE AWAY FROM ME?
FAMILY... SURVIVED THE CRASH... THEY'RE HERE... ON THE ISLAND...

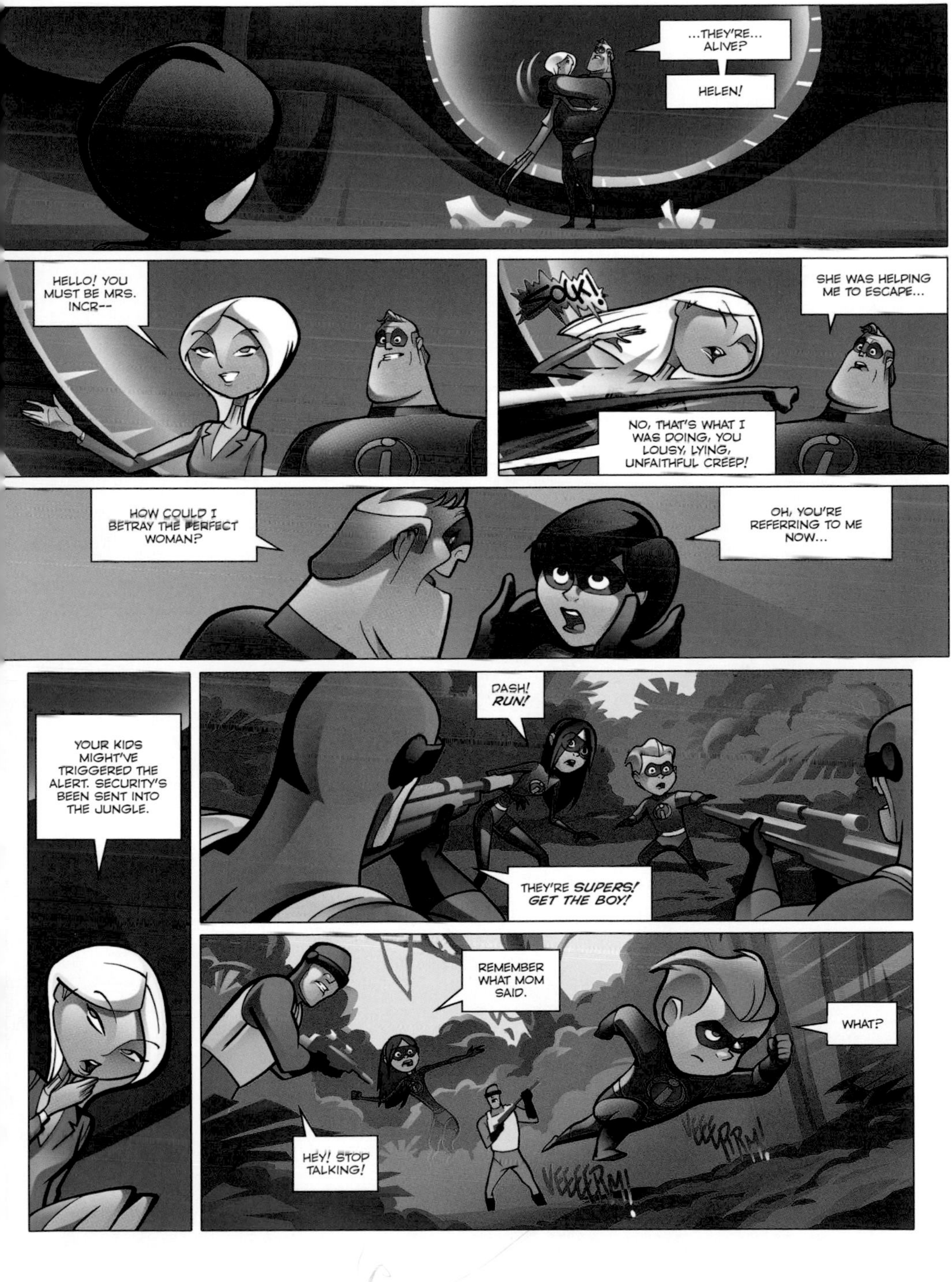
...THEY'RE... ALIVE?
HELEN!
HELLO! YOU MUST BE MRS. INCR--
SOCK!
SHE WAS HELPING ME TO ESCAPE...
NO, THAT'S WHAT I WAS DOING, YOU LOUSY, LYING, UNFAITHFUL CREEP!
HOW COULD I BETRAY THE PERFECT WOMAN?
OH, YOU'RE REFERRING TO ME NOW...
YOUR KIDS MIGHT'VE TRIGGERED THE ALERT. SECURITY'S BEEN SENT INTO THE JUNGLE.
DASH! RUN!
THEY'RE SUPERS! GET THE BOY!
REMEMBER WHAT MOM SAID.
WHAT?
HEY! STOP TALKING!
VEEEERRM!
VEEEERRM!

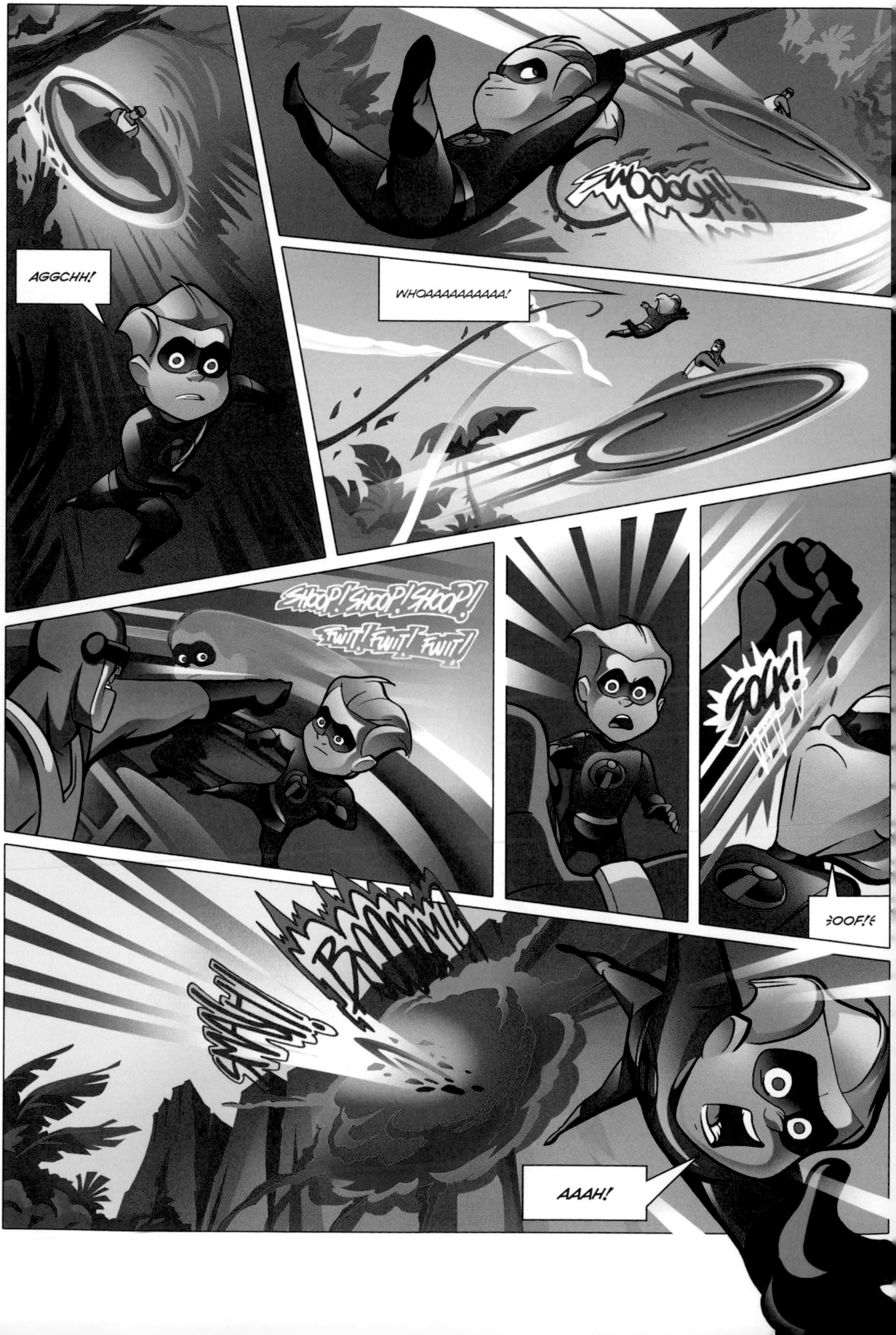
SWOOOSH!
AGGCHH!
WHOAAAAAAAAAA!
SHOOP! SHOOP! SHOOP!
FWIT! FWIT! FWIT!
SOCK!
OOF!
BOOOM!
SMASH!
AAAH!

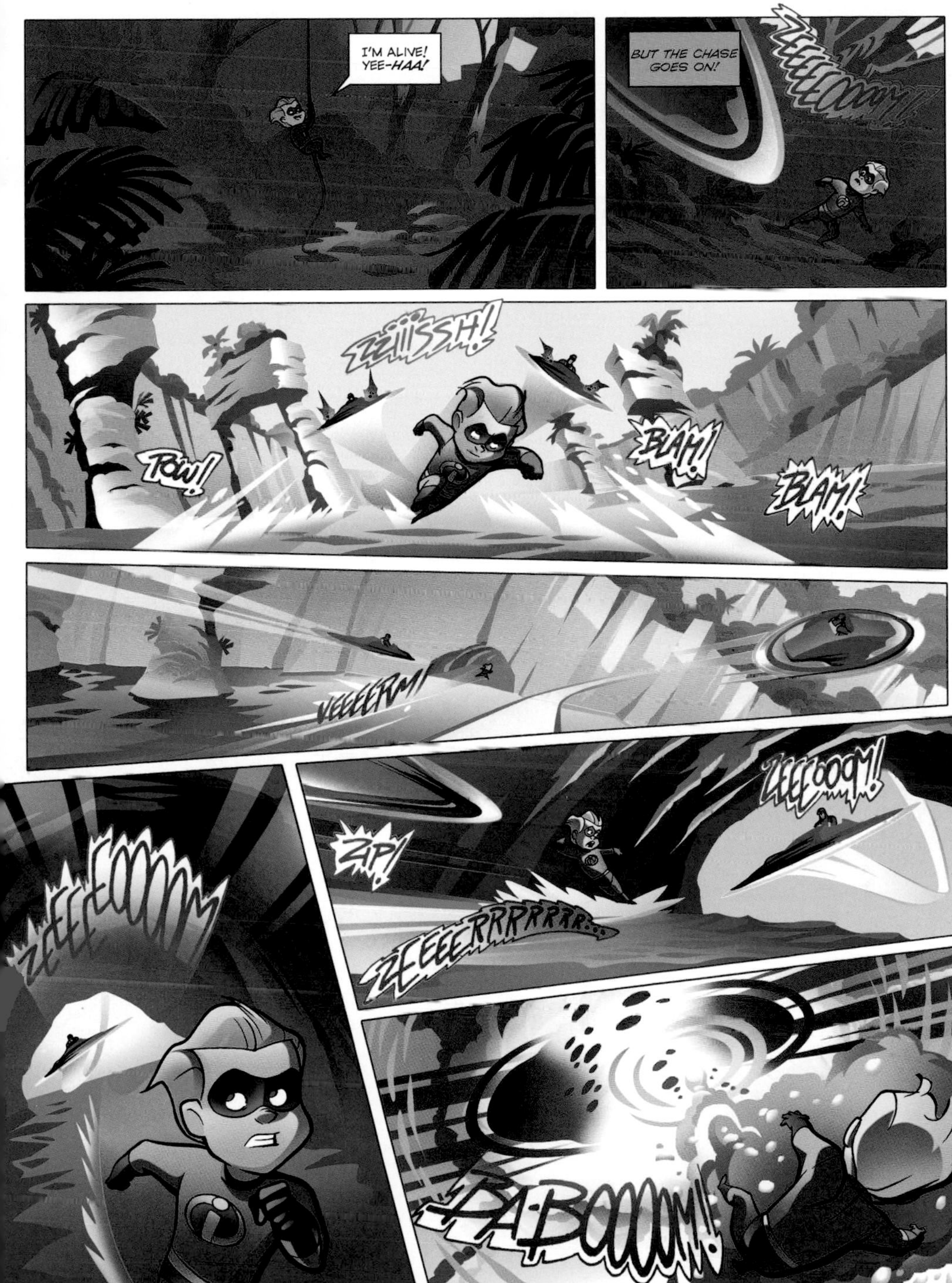
I'M ALIVE! YEE-HAA!
BUT THE CHASE GOES ON!
ZEEEEOOOM!
ZZIIISSH!
POW!
BLAM!
BLAM!
VEEEERM!
ZEEEEOOOM
ZIP!
ZEEEOOOM!
ZEEEERRRRRRR...
BA-BOOOOM!

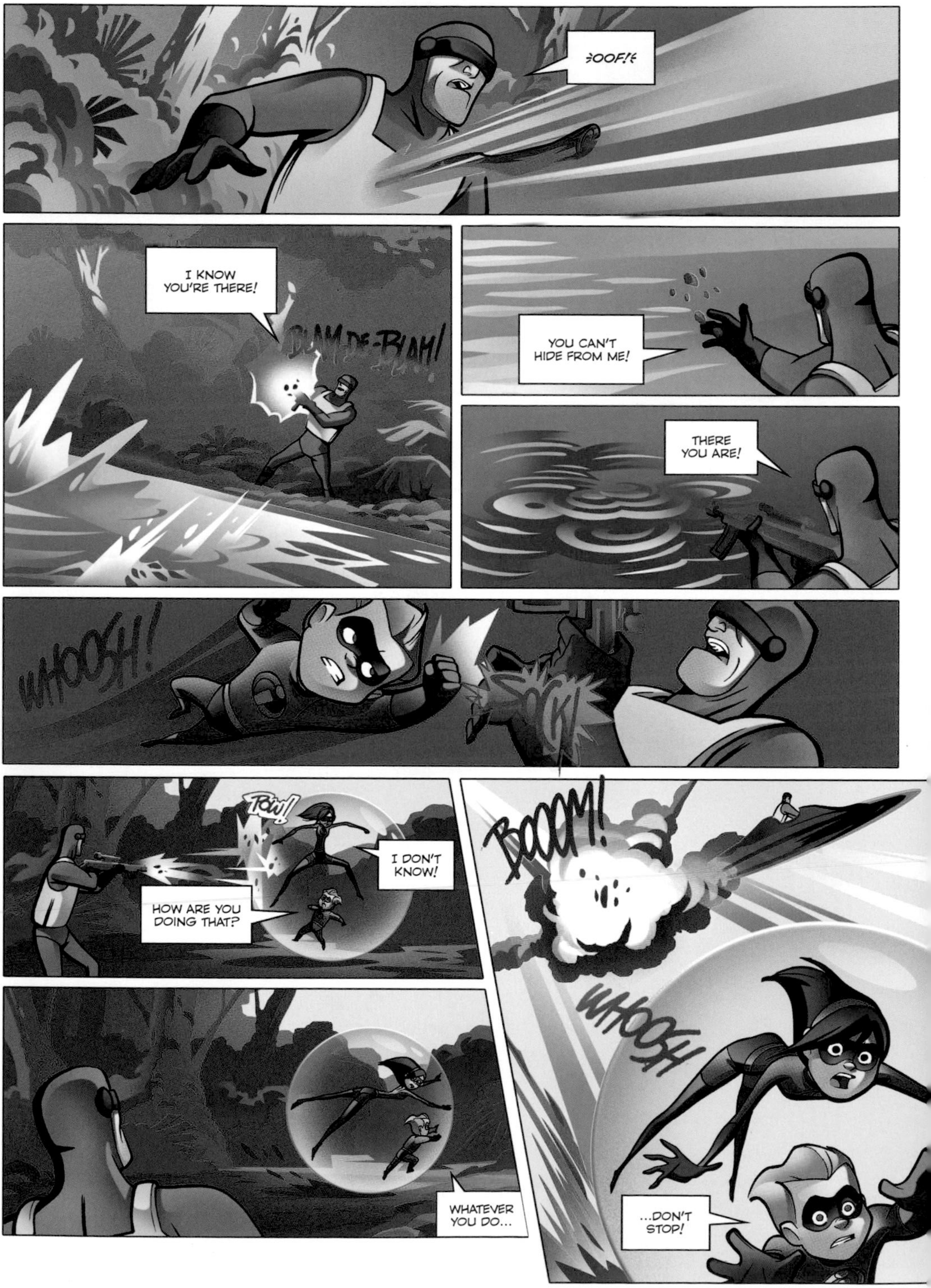
OOF!
I KNOW YOU'RE THERE!
BLAM-DE-BLAH!
YOU CAN'T HIDE FROM ME!
THERE YOU ARE!
WHOOSH!
SOCK!
POW!
I DON'T KNOW!
HOW ARE YOU DOING THAT?
BOOOM!
WHOOSH
WHATEVER YOU DO...
...DON'T STOP!

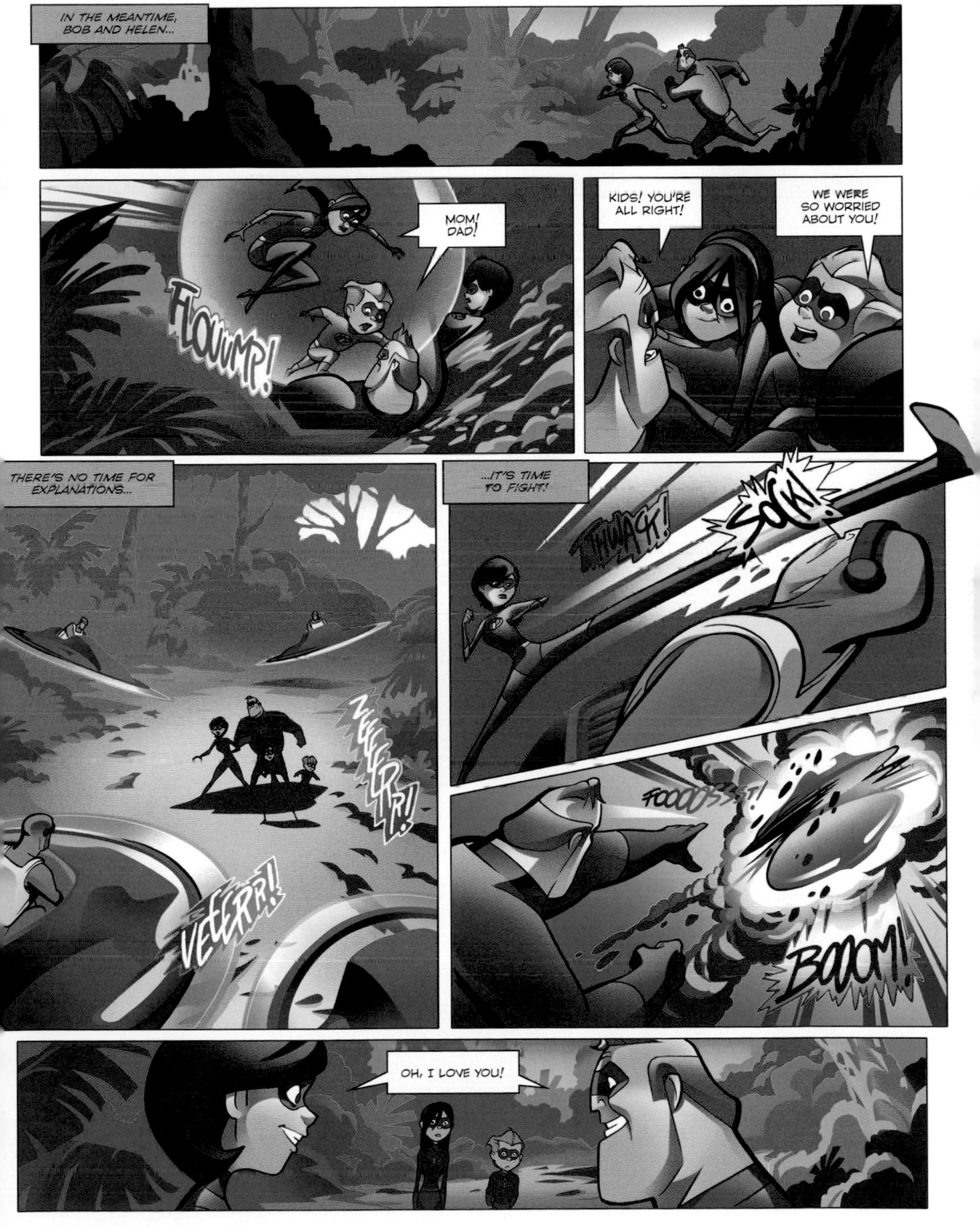
IN THE MEANTIME, BOB AND HELEN...
FLOUUMP!
MOM! DAD!
KIDS! YOU'RE ALL RIGHT!
WE WERE SO WORRIED ABOUT YOU!
THERE'S NO TIME FOR EXPLANATIONS...
ZEEEERR!
VEEERRR!
...IT'S TIME TO FIGHT!
THWACK!
SOCK!
FOOOOSSST!
BOOOM!
OH, I LOVE YOU!

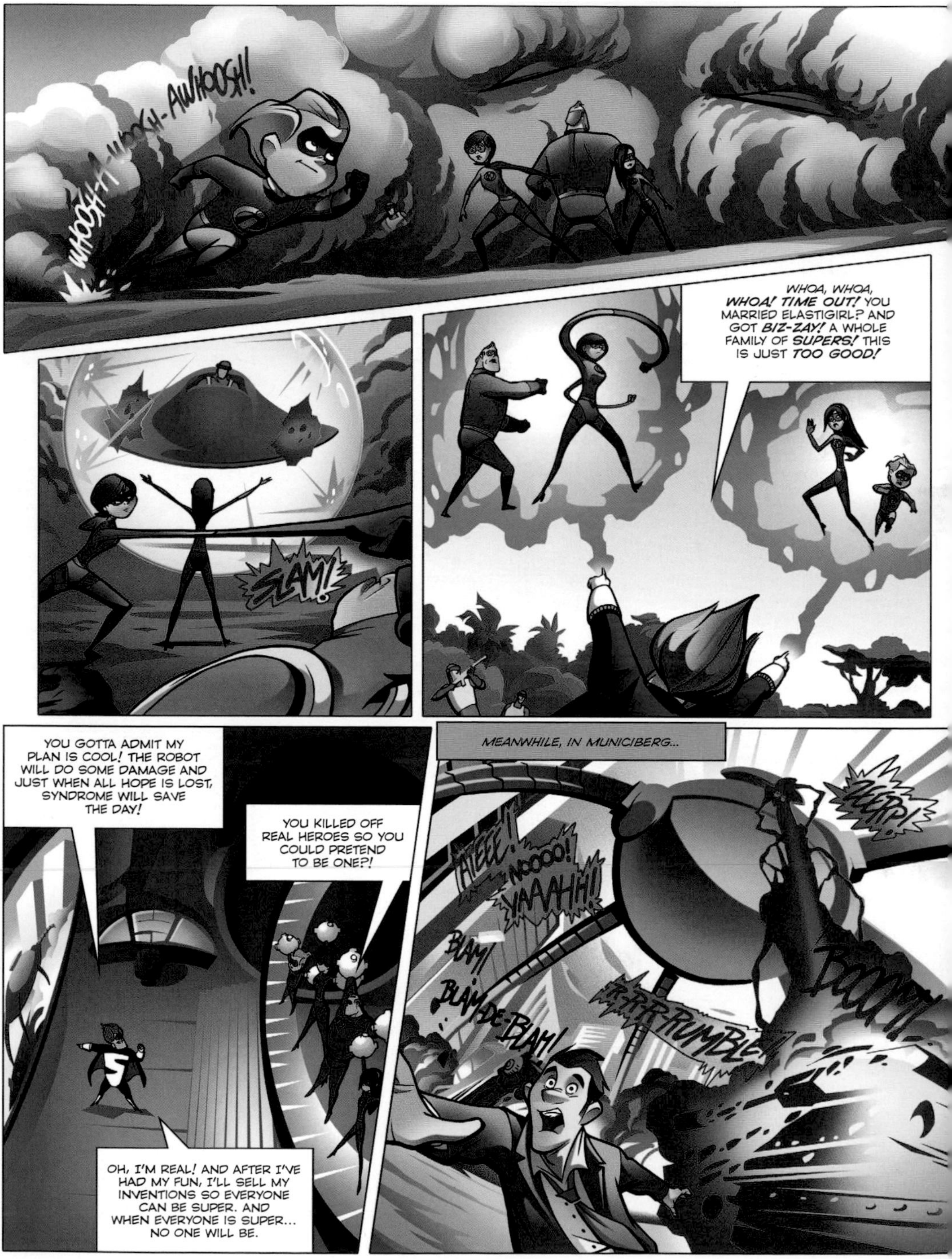
WHOOSH-A-WHOOSH-AWHOOSH!
SLAM!
WHOA, WHOA, **WHOA! TIME OUT!** YOU MARRIED ELASTIGIRL? AND GOT ***BIZ-ZAY!*** A WHOLE FAMILY OF ***SUPERS!*** THIS IS JUST ***TOO GOOD!***
YOU GOTTA ADMIT MY PLAN IS COOL! THE ROBOT WILL DO SOME DAMAGE AND JUST WHEN ALL HOPE IS LOST, SYNDROME WILL SAVE THE DAY!
YOU KILLED OFF REAL HEROES SO YOU COULD PRETEND TO BE ONE?!
OH, I'M REAL! AND AFTER I'VE HAD MY FUN, I'LL SELL MY INVENTIONS SO EVERYONE CAN BE SUPER. AND WHEN EVERYONE IS SUPER... NO ONE WILL BE.
MEANWHILE, IN MUNICIBERG...
ZEERP!
AIEEE!
NOOOO!
YAAAHH!!
BLAM!
BLAM-DE-BLAM!
R-R-R-RUMBLE!
BOOOM!!

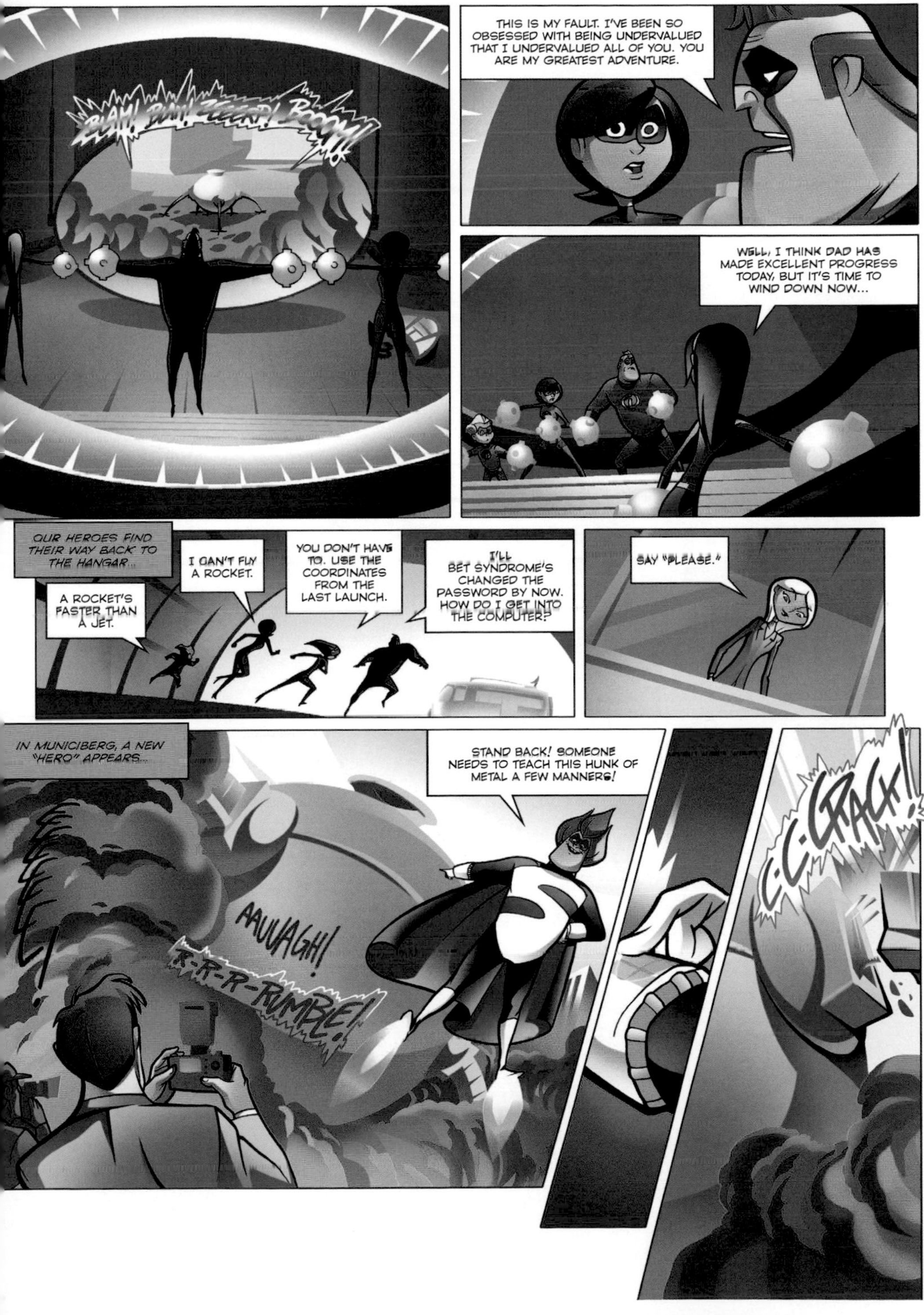
BLAM! BLAM! ZZERP! BOOOM!!
THIS IS MY FAULT. I'VE BEEN SO OBSESSED WITH BEING UNDERVALUED THAT I UNDERVALUED ALL OF YOU. YOU ARE MY GREATEST ADVENTURE.
WELL, I THINK DAD HAS MADE EXCELLENT PROGRESS TODAY, BUT IT'S TIME TO WIND DOWN NOW...
OUR HEROES FIND THEIR WAY BACK TO THE HANGAR...
A ROCKET'S FASTER THAN A JET.
I CAN'T FLY A ROCKET.
YOU DON'T HAVE TO. USE THE COORDINATES FROM THE LAST LAUNCH.
I'LL BET SYNDROME'S CHANGED THE PASSWORD BY NOW. HOW DO I GET INTO THE COMPUTER?
SAY "PLEASE."
IN MUNICIBERG, A NEW "HERO" APPEARS...
STAND BACK! SOMEONE NEEDS TO TEACH THIS HUNK OF METAL A FEW MANNERS!
AAUUAGH!
R-R-R-RUMBLE!
C-C-CRACK!!

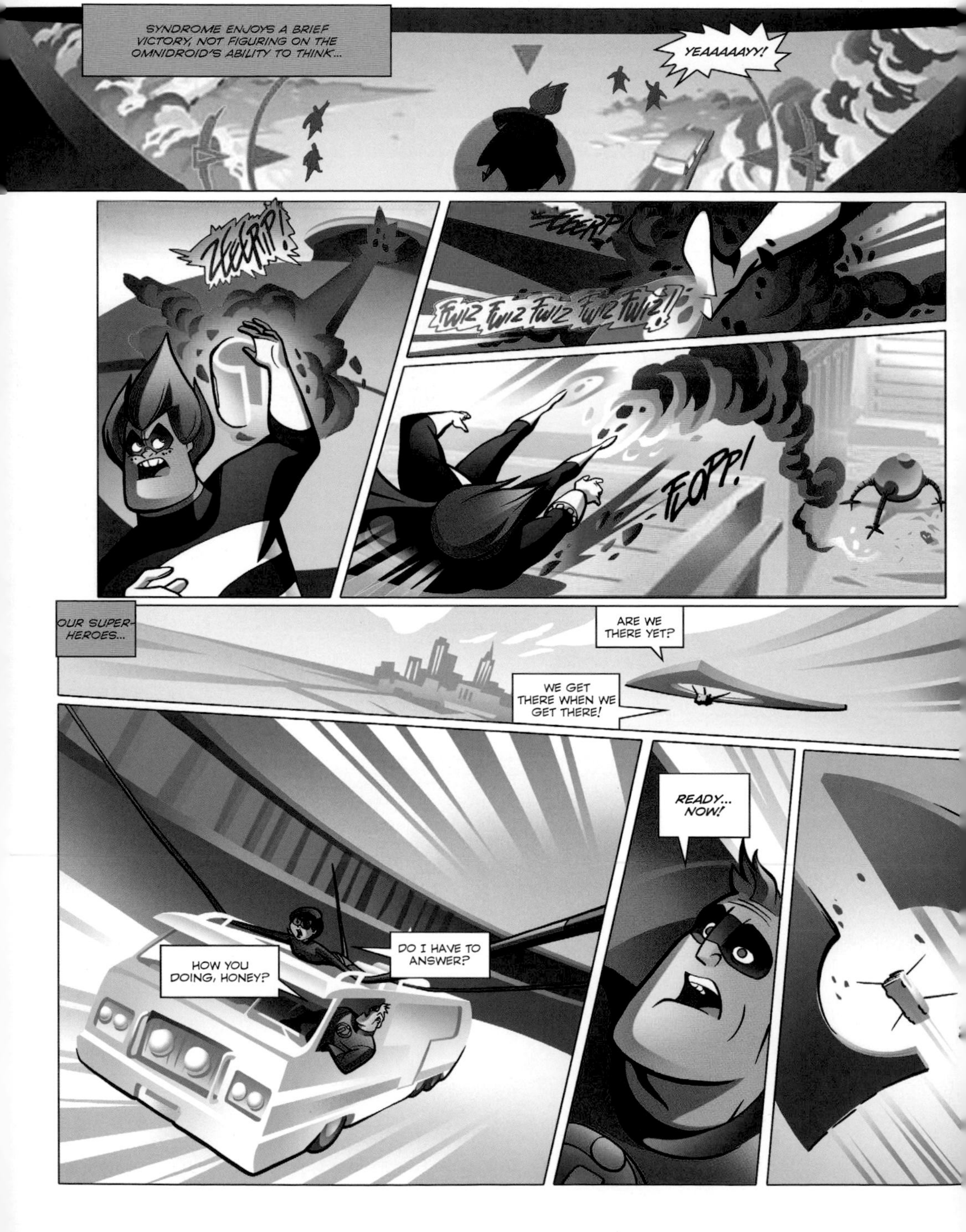
SYNDROME ENJOYS A BRIEF VICTORY, NOT FIGURING ON THE OMNIDROID'S ABILITY TO THINK...
YEAAAAAYY!
ZEEERIP!
ZEEERP!
FWIZ FWIZ FWIZ FWIZ FWIZ!
FEOPP!
OUR SUPER-HEROES...
ARE WE THERE YET?
WE GET THERE WHEN WE GET THERE!
HOW YOU DOING, HONEY?
DO I HAVE TO ANSWER?
READY... NOW!

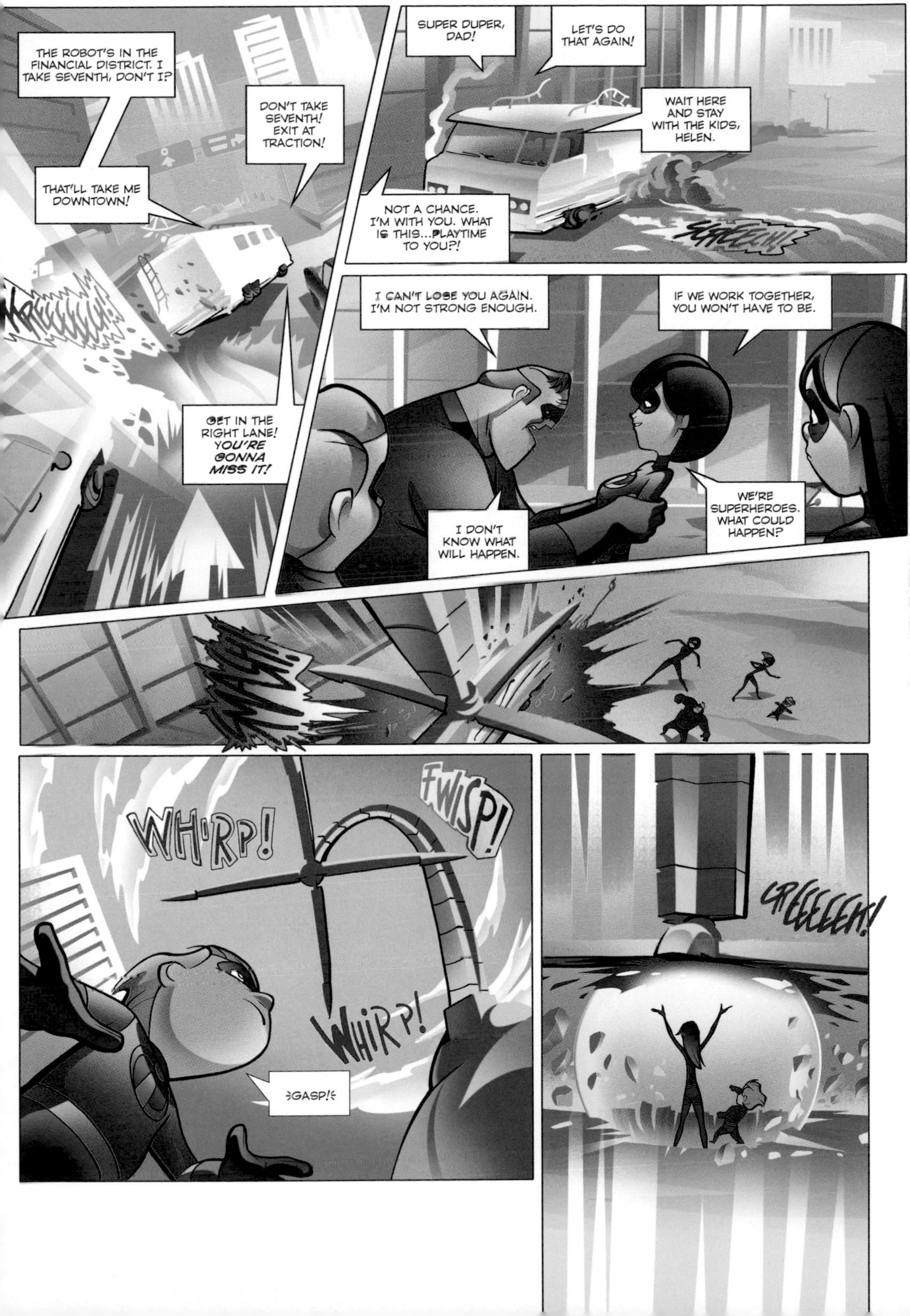
THE ROBOT'S IN THE FINANCIAL DISTRICT. I TAKE SEVENTH, DON'T I?
DON'T TAKE SEVENTH! EXIT AT TRACTION!
THAT'LL TAKE ME DOWNTOWN!
KREEEEEECH!
GET IN THE RIGHT LANE! YOU'RE GONNA MISS IT!
SUPER DUPER, DAD!
LET'S DO THAT AGAIN!
WAIT HERE AND STAY WITH THE KIDS, HELEN.
NOT A CHANCE. I'M WITH YOU. WHAT IS THIS...PLAYTIME TO YOU?!
SCREEECH!
I CAN'T LOSE YOU AGAIN. I'M NOT STRONG ENOUGH.
IF WE WORK TOGETHER, YOU WON'T HAVE TO BE.
I DON'T KNOW WHAT WILL HAPPEN.
WE'RE SUPERHEROES. WHAT COULD HAPPEN?
WHIRP!
FWISP!
WHIRP!
GASP!
GREEEEEEK!

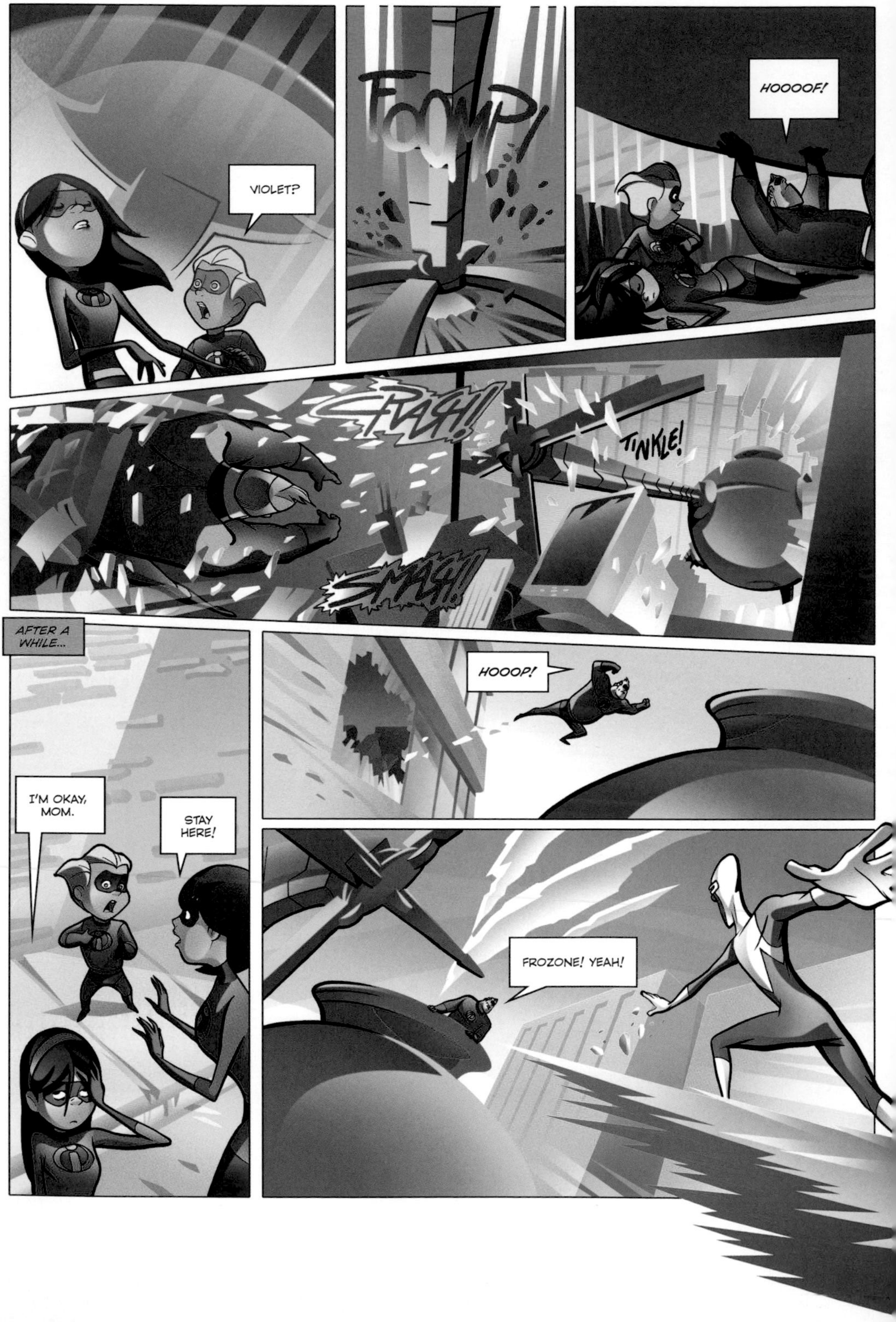

VIOLET?
FOOMP!
HOOOOF!
CRASH!
TINKLE!
SMASH!
AFTER A WHILE...
I'M OKAY, MOM.
STAY HERE!
HOOOP!
FROZONE! YEAH!

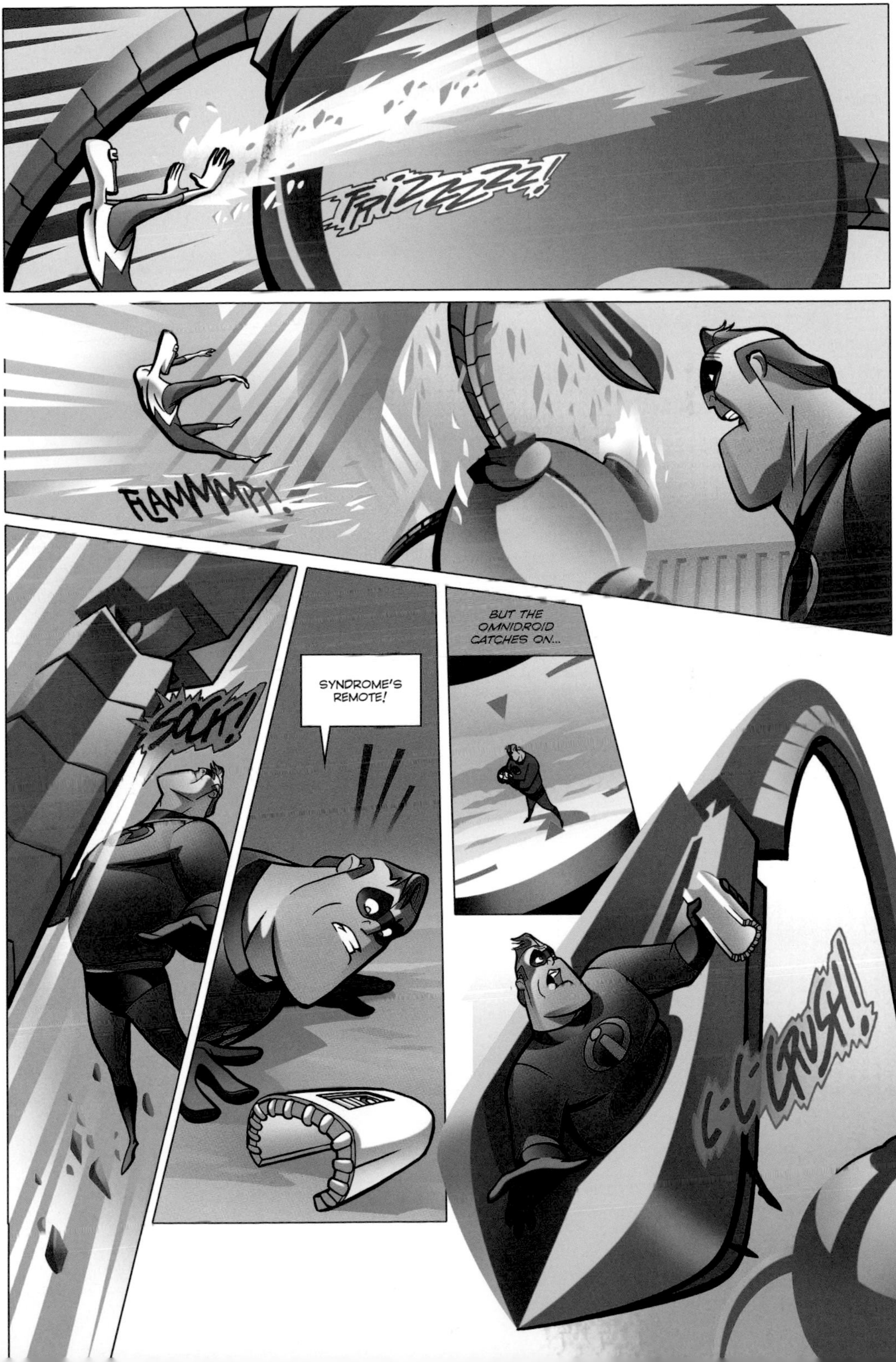
FRIZZZZZZ!
FLAMMMPT!
SOCK!
SYNDROME'S REMOTE!
BUT THE OMNIDROID CATCHES ON...
C-C-CRUSH!

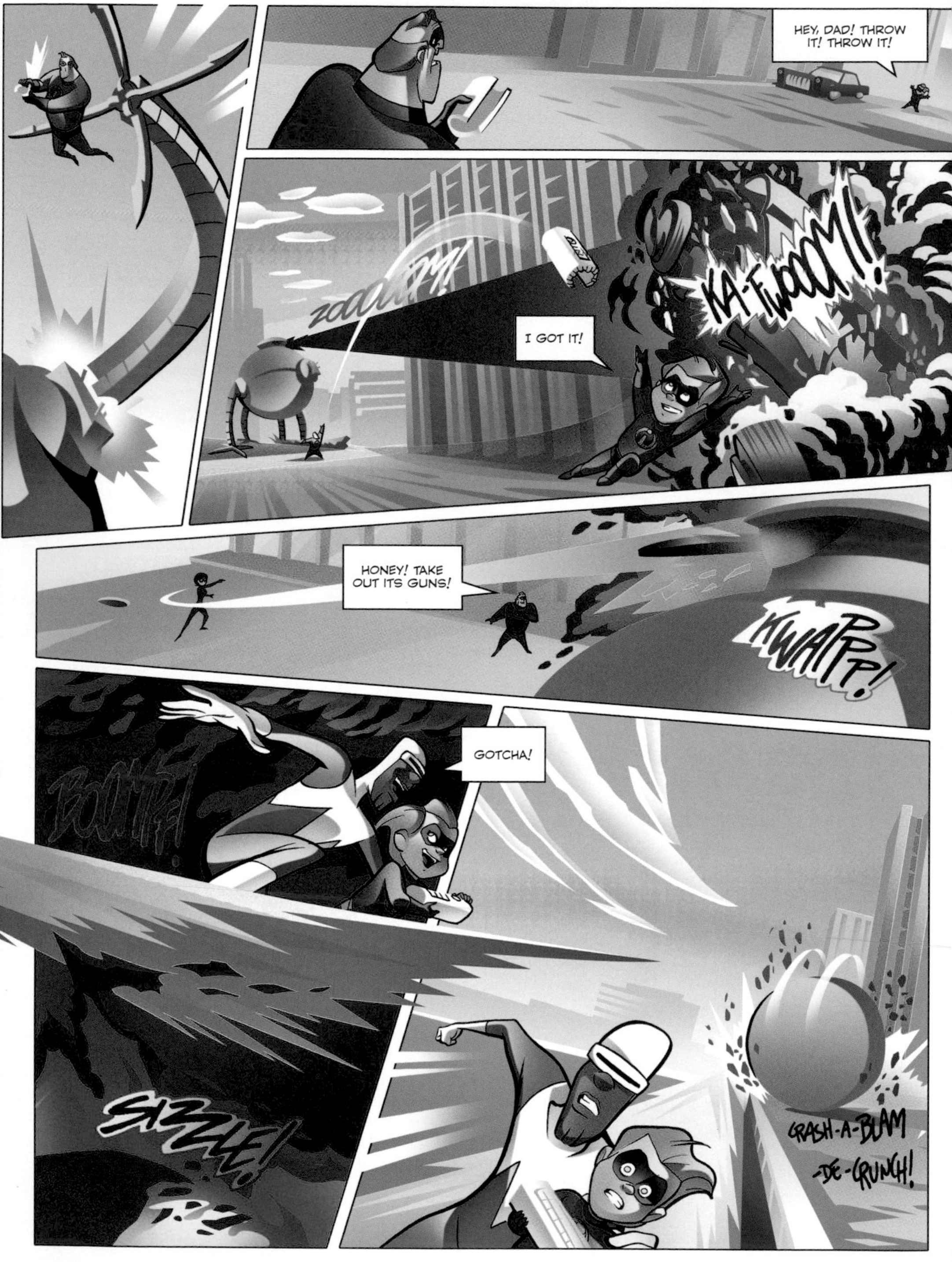

HEY, DAD! THROW IT! THROW IT!
ZOOOOOOM!
KA-FWOOOM!!
I GOT IT!
HONEY! TAKE OUT ITS GUNS!
KWAPPP!
GOTCHA!
SIZZLE!
CRASH-A-BLAM
-DE-CRUNCH!

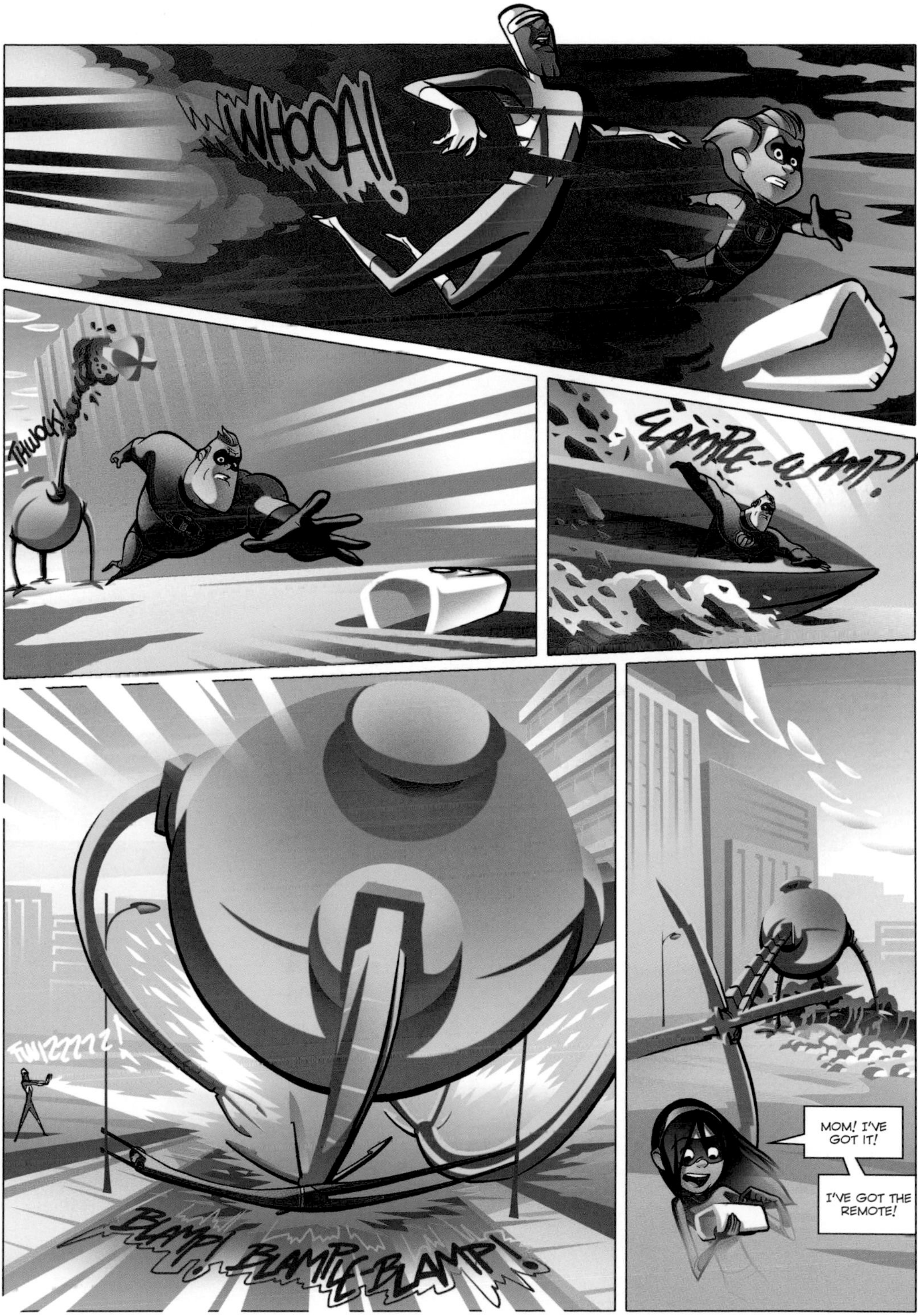
WHOOA!
THWOCK!
CLAMBLE-CLAMP!
FWIZZZZZ!
BLAMP! BLAMPLE-BLAMP!
MOM! I'VE GOT IT!
I'VE GOT THE REMOTE!

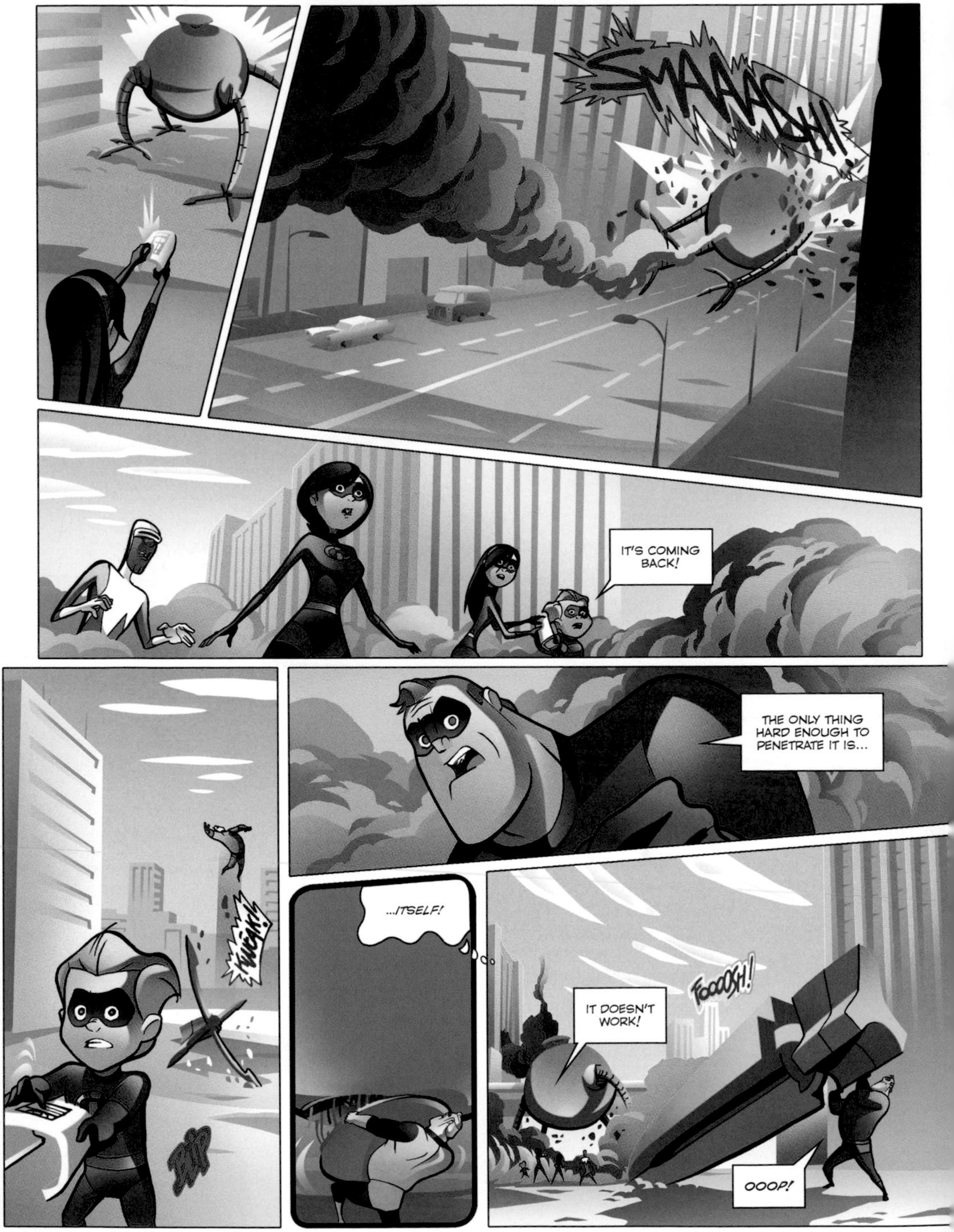
SMAAACH!
IT'S COMING BACK!
THE ONLY THING HARD ENOUGH TO PENETRATE IT IS...
...ITSELF!
IT DOESN'T WORK!
FOOOOSH!
OOOP!

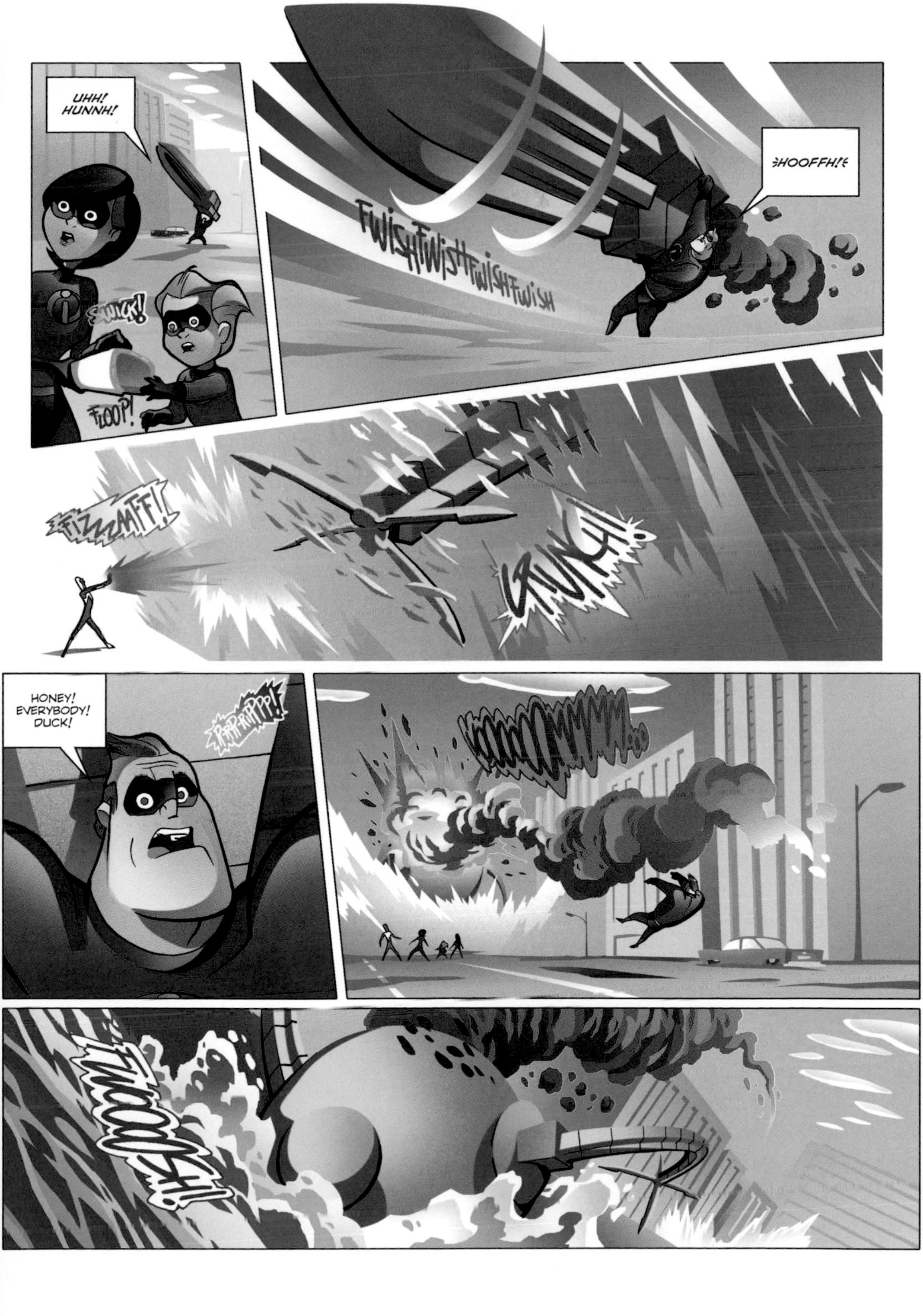
UHH! HUNNH!
SHLUCK!
FLOOP!
FWISHFWISHFWISHFWISH
HOOFFH!
FIZZZAAFF!
HONEY! EVERYBODY! DUCK!
RRRP-RIPPPP!
VROOOOMMMM...
FWOOOSH!

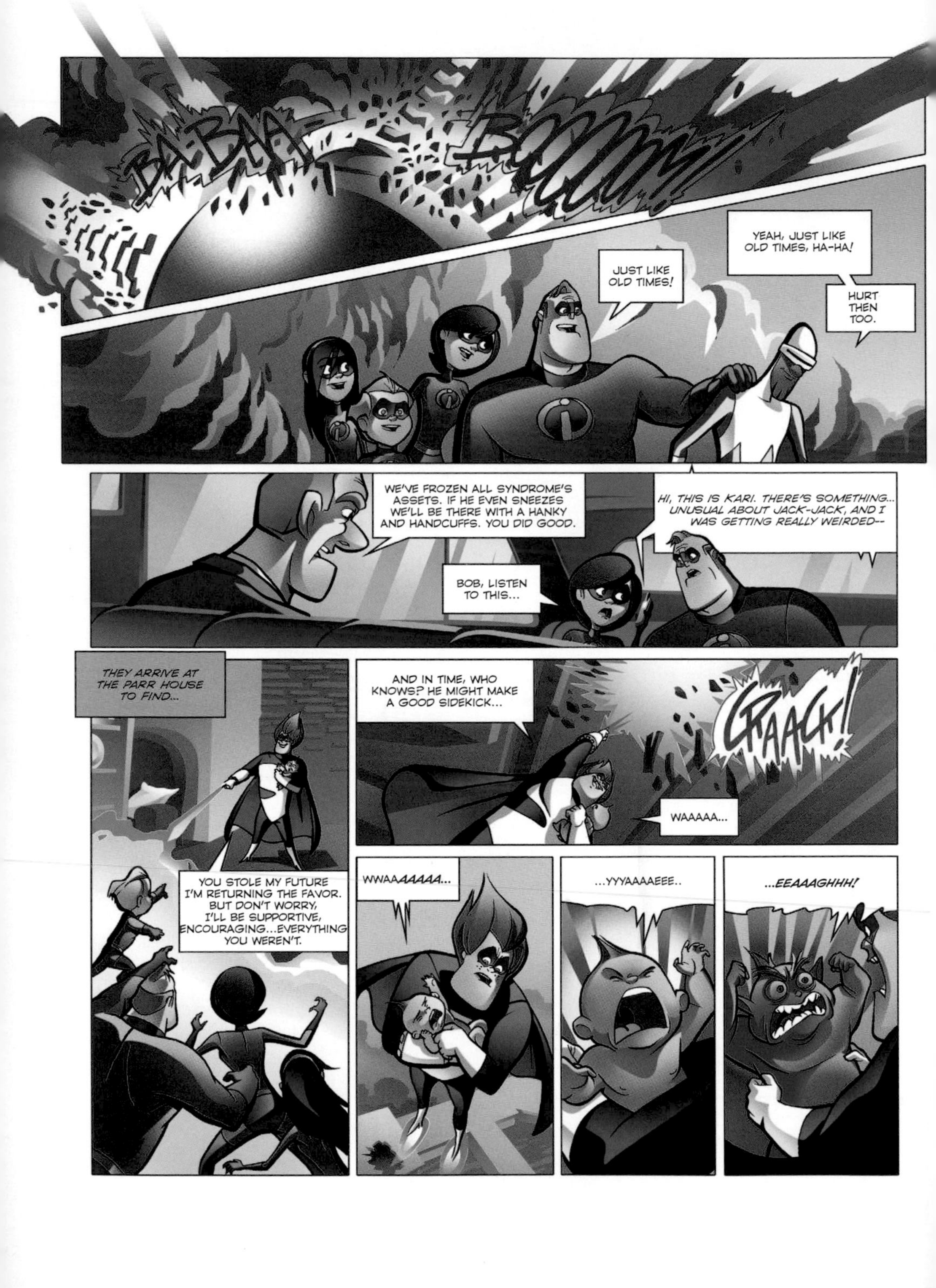
BA-BAA-BOOOOM!
JUST LIKE OLD TIMES!
YEAH, JUST LIKE OLD TIMES, HA-HA!
HURT THEN TOO.
WE'VE FROZEN ALL SYNDROME'S ASSETS. IF HE EVEN SNEEZES WE'LL BE THERE WITH A HANKY AND HANDCUFFS. YOU DID GOOD.
HI, THIS IS KARI. THERE'S SOMETHING... UNUSUAL ABOUT JACK-JACK, AND I WAS GETTING REALLY WEIRDED--
BOB, LISTEN TO THIS...
THEY ARRIVE AT THE PARR HOUSE TO FIND...
YOU STOLE MY FUTURE I'M RETURNING THE FAVOR. BUT DON'T WORRY, I'LL BE SUPPORTIVE, ENCOURAGING...EVERYTHING YOU WEREN'T.
AND IN TIME, WHO KNOWS? HE MIGHT MAKE A GOOD SIDEKICK...
CRAACK!
WAAAAA...
WWAAAAAAAA...
...YYYAAAAEEE..
...EEAAAAGHHH!

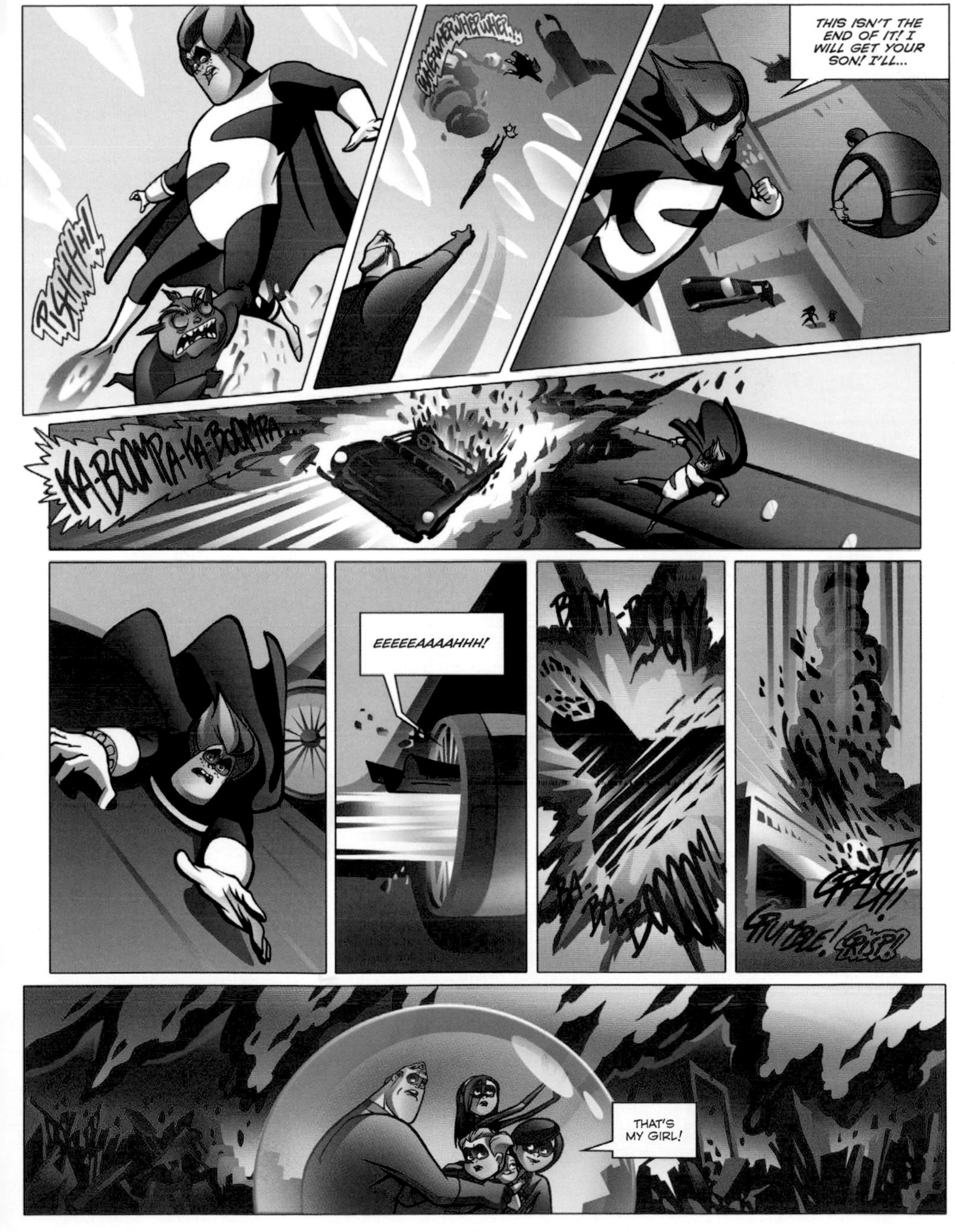
THIS ISN'T THE END OF IT! I WILL GET YOUR SON! I'LL...
KA-BOOMPA-KA-BOOMPA...
EEEEEAAAAHHH!
CRASH!
GRUMBLE!
CRISP!
THAT'S MY GIRL!

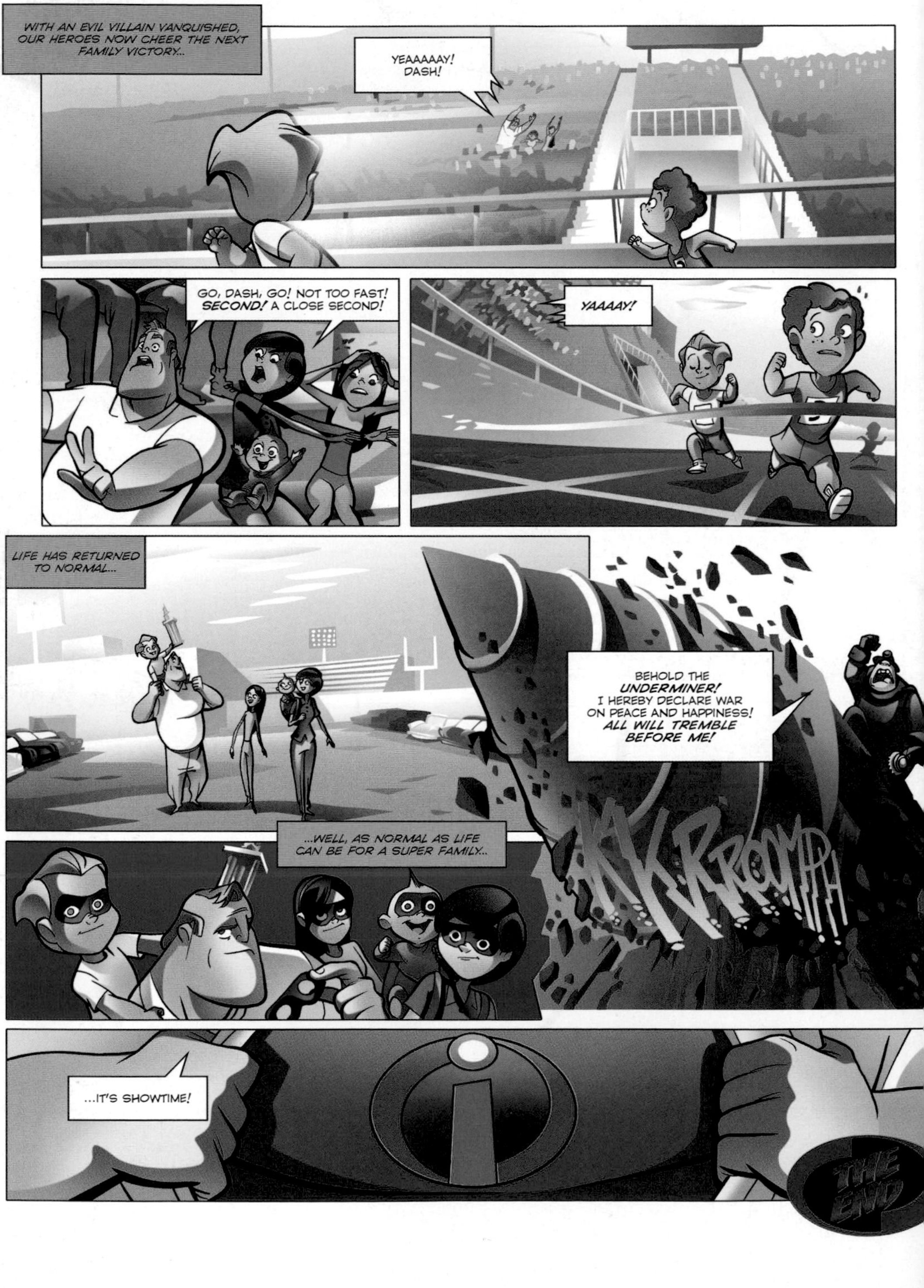
WITH AN EVIL VILLAIN VANQUISHED, OUR HEROES NOW CHEER THE NEXT FAMILY VICTORY...
YEAAAAAY! DASH!
GO, DASH, GO! NOT TOO FAST! SECOND! A CLOSE SECOND!
YAAAAY!
LIFE HAS RETURNED TO NORMAL...
BEHOLD THE UNDERMINER! I HEREBY DECLARE WAR ON PEACE AND HAPPINESS! ALL WILL TREMBLE BEFORE ME!
KKRROOMPH
...WELL, AS NORMAL AS LIFE CAN BE FOR A SUPER FAMILY...
...IT'S SHOWTIME!
THE END

CREDITS

WRITER Gregory Ehrbar

ARTIST Giovanni Rigano

COLOR ARTIST Giorgio Vallorani

DISNEY PUBLISHING WORLDWIDE
Global Magazines, Comics and Partworks

PUBLISHER Lynn Waggoner

EDITORIAL TEAM Bianca Coletti (Director, Magazines), Guido Frazzini (Director, Comics), Carlotta Quattrocolo (Executive Editor), Stefano Ambrosio (Executive Editor), Camilla Vedove (Senior Manager, Editorial Development), Behnoosh Khalili (Senior Editor), Julie Dorris (Senior Editor)

DESIGN Enrico Soave (Senior Designer)

ART Ken Shue (VP, Global Art), Roberto Santillo (Creative Director), Marco Ghiglione (Creative Manager), Stefano Attardi (Computer Art Designer), Manny Mederos (Creative Manager)

PORTFOLIO MANAGEMENT Olivia Ciancarelli (Director)

BUSINESS & MARKETING Mariantonietta Galla (Marketing Manager), Virpi Korhonen (Editorial Manager)

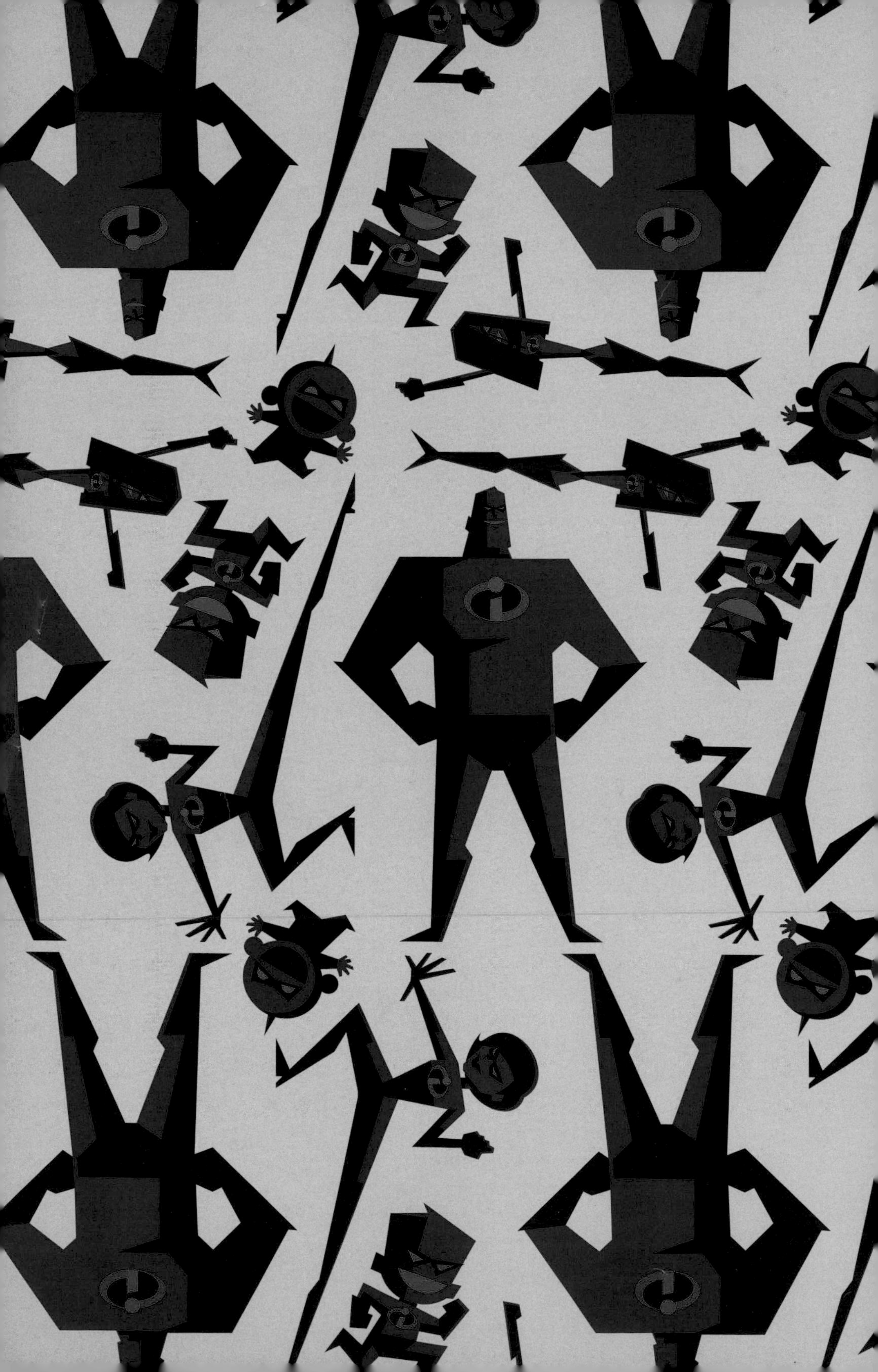